Wolf LEGEND

by

Florence Witkop

Published by Take Me Away Books, a division of Winged Publications

ISBN-13: 978-1-946939-33-3
ISBN-10: 1-946939-33-1

Chapter One

"You're sure you can operate this thing?"

I chose not to be insulted though it was hard. Dr. Portman, good looking though he was, wasn't endearing himself to me, but I gritted my teeth and told myself he was probably one of those people who can't handle last-minute changes so being irritable wasn't truly his fault. I had to force a smile but I'd be living with the guy for a week, I kept telling myself that he was normally nice.

To be honest, Will and Jake coming down with a flu that was going around qualified as enough of a major last-minute change to cause any landlubber to panic because it meant my strapping brothers couldn't take the professor to the island after all and I'd be filling in.

Me. Just me. All five feet and barely something more of me and that must look pretty puny to someone who'd been expecting them. No six foot something each of my two brothers who were guys who could wipe the floor with anyone who looked at them sidewise and who were capable of handling any emergency imaginable. The guys the good professor expected to be waiting at the dock.

So maybe I wasn't what was expected when he showed up complete with a backpack so new it squeaked and hiking boots that weren't even close to being broken in. His feet would hurt before the week was over.

I stopped stowing gear long enough to give the good professor as hard a stare as possible, something I'm rather good at. After all, I've lived with my brothers my whole life. Through necessity, I've learned a thing or two about bluffing.

Remembering all those years and lessons learned, I folded my arms and let my whole self go still to show him how confident I was of my ability to guide and care for a city-bred college professor for a whole week on an inhabited island. I lifted my chin and prepared to stare him down. "I'm as good as Will and Jake any day. Better."

Jake snorted into his sleeve and Will turned away so the good professor wouldn't see his laugh. But I can handle the Delight as well as anyone in my family and that's saying a lot because we Petersons have been making a nice piece of change taking our various fishing boats onto Lake of The Woods for generations.

Okay, we mostly farm, but we've been on the big lake enough to know storm clouds when we see them, and how to get the hell off the water in a hurry, and where northerns and walleyes hang out so we can get fishermen to the right spot at the right time and just about guarantee that they catch their limit and brag about it. And afterwards, with their stringers hanging heavy, we remind them to refer their friends to us for future fishing trips. They usually do.

It's a nice gig and Will and Jake weren't about to take a chance on having the good professor bad-mouth our business because they got sick. Even though he wasn't hiring the Delight and crew for a fishing trip, word would get around if the professor was unhappy. Fishermen would hear and avoid us like the plague. Of course, he wouldn't be commenting on the size of fish he caught because the good professor wasn't after fish. He was looking for wolves.

Non-existent wolves.

Direwolves, actually, except there aren't any more of them around. Thousands of years ago, yes. Today? Just legends. But I'd spent the last weekend helping spread the word to tourists that huge wolves wander the woods so I wasn't about to argue with the good professor when he said he wanted to check out the legend. I merely nodded, hid my smirk behind my hand and agreed that a week or two on the island in question was a good investment on the part of the nearby wolf center.

Dr. Portman stared hard at my brothers who are normally so healthy they wouldn't look sick if they were dying. "You don't look sick to me."

"They are." How dare he question Will and Jake? Being a popular professor didn't give him the right to criticize my family. I went to their defense. "They stuffed enough over-the-counter medication into their bodies to put lesser people in the drunk tank in order to be able to stagger to the dock this morning and make sure we have everything we need for a week on the island. And to meet you as promised and tell you I'm the substitute. And to help us cast off, even though they should be in bed."

Just then, Will started coughing and he wasn't joking. Dr. Portman backed away and looked a bit abashed. "Sorry. You should be home in bed." He raked fingers through his hair. Thick hair but short, it was the same sandy color as both of my brothers had, though he was from New York instead of the wilds of the north woods. And blocky where they were long and lanky, which made him even more impressive and people remember Will and Jake when they go anywhere together.

Looking him over covertly, I decided I like blocky. "I'm sure your sister will do just fine." He turned to me, started to say something, then stopped and I realized we hadn't been introduced. "Jane. My name's Jane." I stuck out a hand and he took it.

As we shook hands, I knew he didn't recognize me. I was a student at Weatherby College where he taught, and I'd be a senior come fall. I'd spent three years walking past his office every single day but now he didn't know me from Adam.

His handshake was firm, I gave him that. And warm. "Buck." So he had a first name and I wasn't expected to call him Dr. Portman while on the island where we wouldn't find any wolves. But of course I'd call him Dr. Portman when the school year started.

Will and Jake shoved us off and stood on the dock until we were out of sight, coiling ropes and watching their baby sister point the Delight towards an island so insignificant it didn't even have a name.

Not too many hours later, I nosed the Delight towards the protected side of the island, back trolling to brake its too-fast forward thrust until it bumped gently against an evergreen that had somehow managed to thrive in pure granite.

Dr. Portman ... Buck... quickly threw a rope around the largest branch and snugged it tight, looking all kinds of athletic in the process. So he wasn't helpless after all. Not quite, anyway. I'd yet to see how he fared in the thick forest that covered the island.

The island itself was larger than expected. Maybe it had a name after all, though everyone I'd asked simply referred to it as the island that was an hour south of a sand bar where walleyes abounded.

By the time we'd unloaded a couple week's worth of camping equipment, I knew why that tree was so healthy. Somewhere on the island, I couldn't see where, a rising spring carried life-giving dirt and other detritus through the forest. It then pooled in a depression in that granite boulder and spread over the tree's roots to feed them before falling in a wide sheen over the rock and into Lake of The Woods.

There was no water now. No detritus. The depression that should be a river was dry as a bone because we were in the grip of the worst drought in decades. Everything was dry. The forest floor would crunch and crack beneath our feet, ready to ignite at the touch of a match or the lick of a stray ember. I wondered if the tree would survive the drought. I hoped so.

I stared at the dry forest. "No campfires for the duration of our stay."

Dr. Portman … Buck, I must remember to call him Buck … nodded. "No problem. It's warm." He spread his arms to absorb the sun's rays. On the prow of the Delight, in full sun, he resembled a golden statue and, like a statue, for the moment before he moved, he was beautiful.

I, on the other hand, jumped ashore and was instantly in the forest, in the shade and didn't resemble a goddess at all as I stared at his bulky form. Where my brothers were all length and legs and arms, he'd fit right in with any football team. I was curious. When we were settled and looking for something to talk about I'd ask if he'd ever been a quarterback. Or, more likely, a fullback.

I mentioned the lack of campfire again after an argument with my conscience because he might just be a decent person after all and maybe I'd be glad later if I was honest. "It'll be chilly at night. We'll miss a campfire." Then curiosity got the best of me and I decided not to wait to ask. "Did you play football in college?"

"Didn't have time for sports. I worked my way through college and am just now finishing paying off my loans." He grabbed a duffle bag. "I brought warm clothes." He jumped ashore, joining me in the shade, and his golden glow was instantly muted though in some corner of my mind I knew I'd always think of him that way. In the sun, glowing gold. "No fire is okay with me."

"A fire would keep wolves away." I couldn't help adding, "If there are any on the island."

"I hope there are. I hope I'm not making this trip for nothing."

I didn't answer. Didn't want him leaving the day he arrived. Didn't want him to know that we were on an island that couldn't possibly support even one normal sized wolf, let alone the huge wolves of the legends and he should know that, any wolf researcher should. Unless he wanted to believe. Unless he did know but was willing to put aside his knowledge about wolves in the hope that this one time, there would be wolves where they shouldn't exist. Mostly, I said nothing because I didn't want to lose a sizable chunk of my next year's tuition because that's what his fee would be.

We looked for a place to make camp. Since the island was larger than I'd realized, there were several good spots, but we settled for an open, level spot near the boat because, with the single stream on the island dried up, the lake would be our only source of water. I shivered, thinking how cold that water would be, even in high summer.

It took forever to pitch the tent. My brothers believe in comfort, so a larger-than-necessary outfitters' tent was their choice. Me, I'd choose a tent according to ease of pitching but I knew I'd like the roomy interior once it was up. Standing up in a tent is an enviable luxury. A folding table and chairs in front of the tent became our kitchen and dining room. No fire pit so, before the sun began sliding down to meet the horizon, instead of looking for firewood, we went looking for wolves.

I'm practically an expert on walking quietly through the woods thanks to two brothers who like venison and deer hunting. But silence on that trek was impossible. Dry leaves crunched, and pine twigs snapped with our every step. Dust rose from a forest floor that was inches deep in loam that had accumulated over thousands of years. Beneath the loam was the granite that was the bedrock of the island. Over that loam were towering evergreens and birches, all now showing the effects of the drought.

We walked through a forest without the wolves I pretended to look for. Except ... I saw something caught on a bush. Reached out. Pulled it free. "Fur." I held it up.

He pounced on it. Brought it close to his eyes to see it better. Waved it triumphantly. "There are wolves here after all. I knew it!"

"Could be from a dog."

"On a remote island? No way."

"A fisherman could have stopped for lunch and let his dog run."

His shoulders slumped, then straightened. "It doesn't look like anyone was here."

I looked around. Virgin forest met my eyes. "They could have tied up their boat on the other side of the island."

"Maybe." His eyes were bright with excitement. "Or there could be wolves here, like people say. There's got to be something behind the stories." The story, singular, because it was the same one I'd heard since I was a kid and repeated many times. A legend for tourists.

But I didn't say that, instead I listened to him go on about wolves. "Let's keep going. Maybe we'll find tracks. Tracks will say something." He started off, stopped, looked back at me, and said, "Sorry, I wasn't thinking. It's too dry for tracks, the ground is rock hard. So thanks for the fur. I'd have missed it."

We found two other pieces of fur, sending Buck into overdrive. I mumbled something about dog fur and made sure he heard so when we didn't find wolves he'd know where the fur came from. I didn't mention that no dog was likely to wander far enough from its owner during a lunch stop to leave patches of fur in all the places we found them. But a wolf? Impossible.

Buck didn't stop talking as I cooked dinner on the camp stove and it was all about wolves. "They are ancient, you know." I mentioned that I did know that but he was already talking again. "Dogs are descended from wolves. They can interbreed." I knew that too and mentally tuned him out as I plastered an interested expression on my face while the sun washed the water red to the west and the moon slipped behind the trees in the east, splashing silver here and there though everything around us was black with mere slivers of silver slicing the black void into sections.

That black and silver night crept along the ground towards us, finally chasing evening away and enveloping Buck. He became indistinguishable from the forest except for his voice, a surprisingly mellow baritone that was a melody to the harmony of the night birds and somehow, I found myself actually listening. His speech was companionable, a bulwark against the loneliness of the remote island and I gladly listened to him drone on about wolves until we turned in.

In the morning, that baritone wasn't so mellow. A cough in the sleeping bag on the other side of the tent woke me. I sat up quickly. "Are you okay?"

"It's nothing. I'm probably allergic to something."

"When my brothers first got sick, they coughed just like you."

"I'm the healthiest person on the planet."

"I didn't bring antibiotics."

He jumped up and into his clothes in one huge leap to prove he wasn't sick. I lay back a while longer and privately admired his solid body as I tried to decide what a sick customer would mean to my finances. Dare I ask for full payment if we went home early, or should I accept partial payment because he didn't get his money's worth? Was college tuition more important than being fair?

I groaned and wished I wasn't such an upstanding, honest person. Then I covered my head with a pillow and ignored the question by grabbing another few minutes of sleep. When I emerged ten minutes later, breakfast was waiting.

How could I ask someone who cooked bacon and eggs to perfection to pay full price if they became sick and had to leave early? Especially someone who didn't look all that healthy in the glaring light of morning, in spite of that tough, football player's physique. Dark shadows beneath his eyes said he should have slept late instead of me.

"Want to take it easy today?" I tried to gauge his state of health and failed completely. I'm clueless where illness is concerned, one reason I didn't go into nursing as my parents suggested. "Stick around camp and listen?" Because wolves howl. At the Weatherby College wolf center, which Buck was a part of, people came just to listen to them howl. They thought it was wonderful. I thought it was loud. "If they howl, we can go towards the sound."

He danced around the stove, trying to look fit and athletic and almost succeeding. But then, I'm a sucker for guys who won't wimp out. Guys like Buck as he shook his head. "I'm for looking instead of listening. But if we don't find any sign today, maybe tomorrow we can try something different."

So we slogged through the forest once more only this time we found no fur, nothing to suggest any large carnivores had ever set foot on the island. I didn't look as hard as I might have because I was occupied with watching Buck slowly develop what I now knew was the same bug that had laid my brothers low.

By the time we gave up for the day, I was glumly saying goodbye to a hefty fee for a week of wilderness adventure and wolf hunting. We'd head home in the morning. Buck had other ideas. "No virus will get the best of me." The refuse-to-wimp-out thing I thought appealing was speaking. *Had* thought was appealing. "I know there are wolves out there."

He wasn't as sick as my brothers, but his eyes were shadowed. Yep he was getting sick. Would be sick in a day or so. "Then you're okay with staying in camp tomorrow and listening while I try to call in a wolf?"

"I guess." His scowl outlined the planes of his cheeks. Then he brightened. "I can call too. I can howl. If even one wolf answers, the rest will chime in." He coughed into his sleeve. Not a bad cough, he wasn't dying. "We'll hear and follow the sound."

"No howling for you. You're sick. Rest your voice." It was already a tad scratchy.

"Yeah. Okay. Guess so." He looked at me with suspicion. "Can you really howl like a wolf? I've never seen you at the center."

As if that was the only place with wolves. "When I was a kid, I once howled a wolf into our back yard."

"How wonderful."

"My folks threatened to throw me out with the trash if I ever did it again."

"You communicated with a wild wolf." Awe filled is voice.

"It took all night to settle down the cattle and my dad figured they were so scared they lost weight. You sell cattle by weight."

"Oh."

I toed the ground, swirling a pattern into the dry pine needles to give myself time to think before speaking. He was my client, after all. But I knew what I was talking about. "Not everyone feels as you do about wolves. Wolves are predators."

"I know that." He raked his hair. I had the

impression he'd had this discussion with many people. "But I work with wolves. I've grown really attached to a couple. Sometimes I forget stuff like that."

The next morning, things went a little slower. Buck only coughed twice during the night. Perhaps he'd only get a light case of flu and a quiet day in camp might get rid of it and we'd be able to stay the full week and do some more exploring in the coming days.

I howled for hours with no answers. Then, leaving Buck to take a nap in the late afternoon, I wandered off and explored the nearby area, also with no luck until I tripped over a root and fell into a pile of pine needles.

I'd been following the dry creek bed and the pine needles were in what would be the middle of the creek during a wet year. Even now, even when the creek was dry, beneath the needles the soil was damp. As I fell, needles flew in every direction, revealing the bottom of the creek bed. And a single set of tracks.

Dog tracks. That must be what they were, one of the larger breeds because no wolf had paws that large and I could only imagine the animal they belonged to. As I measured them against the palm of my hand, memories of the local legends surfaced. The legends that had sent Buck to this island.

Legends of wolves twice the size of the ones that roam the forests now. Dire wolves were the most likely source of the legend, those huge wolves that lived alongside mastodons and saber-toothed tigers. But those animals were extinct now so the tracks must belong to a Great Dane or something even larger if there are dogs larger than Great Danes.

I decided against mentioning the tracks to Buck. I'd agreed to bring him to the island and help him hunt for wolves. But I wouldn't take a sick man on a fruitless quest for something that didn't exist. So I brushed leaves back over the tracks until they were covered and then I returned to camp.

I found Buck awake and feeling good enough to plan the next day's search, which meant we wouldn't go home. He looked almost well so I breathed a sigh of relief and listened to his plans.

"We'll draw a grid on the map of the island. Then we'll search the grid square by square until we find wolves, some sign that they were here, or until I can say with certainty that there aren't any."

I'd be sure to be the one searching the creek bed and I'd make sure to leave the pine needles covering the tracks I'd seen. Searching the island the way he suggested should take three or four days, which would nicely finish up the week's charter and I'd get the full payment and put it towards tuition. I almost purred as the sun started its descent towards the water.

Chapter Two

"No wolves yet." Dr. Portman hugged the sleeping bag close around his shoulders and stared at the setting sun. The temperature was dropping. Though it wasn't cold by any means, the night was going to be cooler than last night or the night before. A surprise, but we were isolated and no communication with the outside world meant no weather forecasts.

Cold enough that I'd miss a campfire, a warm, comforting one that would not only keep dangerous animals at bay but would also keep us warm. Not that there were any dangerous animals nearby. The tracks I'd seen were those of a dog. They had to be dog tracks. The alternative was too scary to think about.

I pulled my thoughts back to the present company and spoke at last because Buck was looking at me, waiting for me to say something, to carry my half of a conversation. "In all honesty, the only surprise will be if we actually find a wolf." I cupped my hands around a cup of steaming coffee and bathed in its heat, swishing it and savoring the smell, breathing in the hot, black beverage. Making it last as long as possible before drinking it down though if I didn't drink it soon it would be as cold as my shivering client.

One more year till graduation. I'd happily guide a lot of people to remote islands on wild goose chases in order to earn money for that last year's tuition. I was almost glad my brothers had gotten sick. But I felt sorry for Buck. For Dr. Portman. I'd have to remember not to call him Buck in the coming school year.

I couldn't blame him for wanting to check out the island after some fishermen spread the word all over town about seeing huge wolves. The legend had been around for a long time but no one I knew had actually seen such a wolf.

That didn't matter to the fishermen. They didn't care if they stretched the truth a bit. But Buck had heard and thought such wolves actually existed. Wanted them to exist.

Like everyone else at the wolf center, he'd be overjoyed if a new type of wolf were found nearby and if the new type should be twice the size of heretofore known wolves, so much the better. Such a discovery would make his career. All their careers.

But I decided that the time for honesty had come. Against all reason, I was actually coming to like Buck Portman. Go figure. "I don't think there are any really any big wolves on this island."

"I know that's what you think." He sighed. "And you may be right. You probably are. Still, I'm glad your brothers let me charter their boat to find out for myself." He stirred the dirt in front of him and sipped his coffee. Grimaced because he was cold. "Though even I realized all along that this could turn out to be no more than a wild goose chase."

I studied him over the rim of my cup. While searching for something to say I considered the moon and stars, the clear sky with no promise of rain whatever which meant no fire, little hot coffee, no decent meals. Then I spoke, again choosing honesty though I wasn't sure why. "I do think that's exactly what this is. A wild goose chase."

"There are a lot of people who'd agree with you, including practically everyone at the wolf center." His shoulders slumped. Then they straightened. "But those fishermen seemed so certain. They even described the color. Silver-black. That's not a color someone would pick from thin air."

He pressed his lips together and his brows knit. "Anyway, I want to know I gave it a good try. I want to either find wolves or prove absolutely that there aren't any." He looked hard in my direction. If the sun was still full, I'd have felt that gaze in every pore. But it wasn't and his features were rapidly blurring as night approached.

I was glad he couldn't see me clearly. It made it easier to talk without worrying about how my words would be received because what I was about to say wasn't what he wanted to hear. "It's not a huge island. Not one with miles and miles of territory." I patiently repeated what I'd learned as a child. "Wolves are predators who can only survive in an area large enough to support a lot of prey animals. Which was why they came to the farm every so often. Why I could call one in. Because their range was decreasing or their family was increasing. More mouths to feed meant more food was needed and our cattle would fill the bill nicely." I mentally pictured the island as we'd seen it thus far. "It isn't large enough to support a wolf pack of normal size let alone one consisting of wolves as large as dire wolves. Think how much prey would be necessary."

"The next few days will tell us."

"I haven't seen signs of other animals. If wolves were on this island and those fishermen truly saw some, it's because they came across on the ice in the winter and were stranded when it thawed. Shortly afterwards, they starved."

"They said they saw wolves last week. Huge wolves, they said. If they were right and there are wolves here, then somehow they found something to eat." He sighed. Rubbed the back of his neck. "But you're probably right."

I felt sorry for him. The life of an assistant professor is one of privation and striving and little chance for advancement in the dog-eat-dog world of the American university system. Finding wolves on this island, especially if they were a variant of known types, would give him a leg up on the competition.

But he should face facts. "It was most likely a big dog. Lots of fishermen take their dogs along. My dad always does, so do my brothers. If one of them stopped here for lunch, he'd let the dog run. Do its business." I shrugged to let him know the subject was closed. "That's what those fishermen saw. Dogs."

He wasn't convinced so I continued. "There have always been rumors about huge wolves in the area. More rumors lately than usual. I've heard them in town. At the feed store." He was listening. "If I'm honest, I'll admit I added to the stories because it was fun to watch the eyes of the tourist next to me. And in the café. And after church when the men talked about their crops and animals and the wolves that preyed on their stock."

"You seem pretty sure it's just gossip."

"I am. Positive." I broached my final argument. My coup. "Because the fishermen mentioned large, healthy wolves." I waved one hand to take in the surrounding trees that somehow had managed to get a foothold in the rocky soil. The needles were turning brown from lack of rain. "This island could never feed a single large wolf, let alone a pack. When those fishermen said they saw several wolves, they were exaggerating for the sake of a good story. They saw one or two dogs. Nothing more, nothing less."

I took a sip of coffee that was quickly growing cold and pretended it was hot as I wrapped my own sleeping bag around my shoulders and waited for the good professor to frown at me. I had, after all, contributed to the gossip that led to his coming to this island and now I was profiting, which made me feel totally guilty. But he said nothing.

It was truly chilly and the professor … Buck … coughed a couple times.

I set the cup on the ground beside me to save the one last cold swallow for later when I turned in for the night. Buck, watching, hooked his own empty cup over his belt and prepared to do the same.

Then something happened. Something impossible.

As my cup touched the ground, the largest wolf I'd ever seen ran through our campsite. Two hundred pounds at least, possibly three hundred, with black velvet, silver-tipped fur and yellow eyes that shone in the night.

It was beautiful. Awesome. And it tore through the camp as if we weren't there, scattering plates and silverware every which way and making short work of the tent just because it happened to be in its path. "Oh dear Lord!" My mouth dropped open because the wolf couldn't exist. Not here, not anywhere. But it did.

The wolf heard. Stopped. Turned towards me. Scared the crap out of me because it was larger than me, double the size of any wolf I'd ever heard of and a predator. Tipped its head to one side and looked straight at me. Stared.

Our looks met. Connected. My fear disappeared because it wasn't looking for food. It was on its way home and in a hurry to get there. The pups missed their mom, the rest of the pack was good, they took care of the pups, but they couldn't take the place of a real mother. It should hurry home.

I blinked. Tried to wrap my mind around what was happening and failed completely.

I couldn't know what it was thinking. I couldn't be reading its mind. Of course not, it was impossible to know what another human being was thinking, let alone a wolf. Wolves were a whole other species. Except that I did.

I was doing precisely what I couldn't do, what no one could do. I was reading its mind and was pretty sure it was reading mine and was just as surprised at being able to read my mind as I was to know what it was thinking. We stared at each other, adjusting to this new reality. Shock kept us both immobile for what seemed like minutes and was probably seconds.

Then the wolf turned away and disappeared into the night because she had a family and responsibilities and couldn't stay to chat, not even for a conversation as mind-blowing as ours. Two separate species were communicating for the first time ever. But she had things to do and places to go, a pack to care for and pups to feed. So she left.

But as she ran into the growing dark, the silver fur blending into the black of the forest, she left a thought behind. "Want to follow me? Want to come for a visit? Maybe we can figure this out."

It was an invitation. One I couldn't turn down.

So I rose and followed the wolf.

Chapter Three

I ran straight into the night. Buck followed, pausing only long enough to grab a flashlight. "I knew it! I knew it! There are wolves on the island. And did you see the size of it? It's huge. It's a behemoth!" He waved the flashlight like a wand until he stumbled. Then he came back to reality and pointed it towards the ground ahead. Then at me. "There are no tracks." Accused me of something, only he didn't know what. I was, after all, going somewhere. "We can't know where it went."

"I know."

He caught up to me. "How?" He looked around. At the blackness that had enveloped us the instant we left the faint reflected light of the lakeshore. In that forest, the dark was complete. Suffocating. Disorienting. "I can't see a thing."

I tried to come up with a rational explanation, something to reassure him. I failed, there was no rational explanation for what I was doing. So I simply said, "It went this way." Then I turned in the direction the wolf had gone and ran into the night.

I wasn't following a sound or a track. Rather I was following a thought. It lingered in the embrace of the trees the way scents do, curling like smoke through air, ready to evaporate or change direction at the first whiff of a breeze, but, also like smoke, it was knowable, identifiable, and easy to follow if I didn't hesitate.

So I charged ahead, disregarding tree roots and twigs that sprang up and tried to trip me. But nothing could stop my headlong dash, nothing could pull me back or slow me down. I was grateful for the flashlight, though at times Buck lagged so far behind that the light wasn't much help.

I ran on, running all out in order to follow my new friend. When we reached my new friend's home and she was able to reassure herself that her pups were fine, we'd figure out what this strange thing was that connected us. Until then, I simply put my head down and ran before the wispy thought that I was following disappeared.

As I ran I realized we were following the dry creek bed. I recognized the pile of pine needles I'd heaped over the wolf tracks to hide them from Buck. When the creek bed turned, so did the wolf spoor and so did we. I wished I'd paid more attention to the layout of the creek as it meandered through the forest. But I hadn't known it would become important so now I had no idea where we were headed and no way of knowing where we were going until we got there.

I'd have run smack into a rock wall if not for Buck's flashlight. As it was, the light showed a cave that must be where the creek originated when there was enough rainfall to fill the creek bed. Buck grabbed me before I could plunge into the cave. "It's the wolf's den. Don't go inside. You'll be attacked. Killed."

No I wouldn't. I wiggled free of Buck's iron grip on my shirt and closed my eyes in order to better concentrate on the thought that I was following. "This isn't the den. That's somewhere else. Farther away."

"Where?" He lifted his hands in question and in sheer bewilderment at my actions. The actions of a crazy woman.

I concentrated harder on the thoughts the wolf had left behind. She'd left them for me so I could find her and I would. "On the other side."

"The other side of what?" He flashed the light upwards. The cave was a hole in a solid granite cliff. It must have taken millions of years for water to grind away enough of the granite to form the cave. He grabbed my shirt, refusing to let me enter what he thought was a dangerous place.

"Let me go." I wiggled until I pulled free.

"What's wrong with you? Don't you want to live? Do you want some mega-wolf to have you for lunch?"

"This isn't the den." I had my shirt back but he held tight to my arm and I couldn't get free. "It's just a creek bed, but if we follow it, we'll find the den on the other side."

He came close and peered into my eyes. We were inches apart as he tried to read my expression in the night and the light of the flashlight. What he saw must have frightened him. "Tell you what. You wait here. I'll climb the boulder. I'll find out what's on the other side." I pulled and twisted but he held me even tighter. "Jane, thanks to you we now know where the wolves live." His words were earnest and caring. "We should go back to camp tonight and return in the morning. We'll find them then but now is suicide. Trust me, I know wolves."

"No!" He didn't understand. "Morning will be too late." The wolf's thoughts were growing weaker as we talked. I was desperate to follow. "The cave goes on practically forever. There are many twists and turns. We must go now before the trail grows cold and I can't follow it."

"What trail?" He flashed the light towards the ground. "There is no trail. No tracks. I don't know how you got this far."

"It's not that kind of trail." I pulled and tugged until I broke free. "I have to go." I evaded his grasp and ran into the cave.

He followed, swearing. "You're going to get us killed." But he kept up as I raced through one room after another in a cave that seemed to go on forever. Until he said, panting, in a kind of wonder, "How big is this cave, anyway? I didn't think the island was this big." Then, in a voice filled with awe, "We must be beneath the lake. That's the only explanation." Then he shut up in order to save his breath because I was getting ahead of him.

As we ran, I got a feel for the way the cave was laid out. Most of it was a blur, but every so often there'd be soft, moist earth beneath our feet which meant we were still following the creek bed. In years of normal rainfall, the cave wouldn't be accessible because it would be full of water. I wondered if we'd find the source of the creek. If we did, would we find wolves waiting for us?

Once, in an area where the cave narrowed, I noticed a piece of fur. Buck saw it too and grabbed it on the run, shoving it into his pants pocket. Proof of wolves on the island. If we didn't find the wolves themselves, the fur could be checked for wolf DNA.

I fleetingly gave Buck credit for more brains than I'd thought when we first met. Then my judgment had been clouded because I'd seen a man who was looking for something that didn't exist. "You were right all along. As were all those people with their stories of huge wolves. Buck, I apologize. The wolves are very real and we are about to meet them on their home turf." I could feel his shudder of fear.

The wolf was fast. I couldn't keep up with her pace. As she got farther and farther ahead of us, her thought trail lessened until, when the cave opened in two different directions, I was forced to stop and concentrate. I looked around. Buck silently handed me the flashlight. He'd figured out that I was following some kind of trail that he couldn't see but that must exist.

I pointed it aimlessly around, hesitating because I wasn't following tracks, I was following thoughts and how could I find a thought with a flashlight? But as the light hit the ground, I knew which way to go because one way went upwards and was dry and dusty-looking, while the other was level and, when I stepped cautiously in that direction, my damp boot print showed clearly. As did the huge paw print next to it. "I guess we go that way," Buck said quietly, between breaths. "Now that we know which way the wolf went, can we rest a bit?"

"No. The trail might go cold."

He took the flashlight and, fatalistically, headed off ahead of me. "You could have said we were following the creek bed. I'd have understood that." He picked up the pace, setting a fast ground-eating trot, showing the way for both of us. "How was I to know that wolves follow creeks?"

"I didn't know myself."

"Then how did you know where the wolf went?" But he didn't wait for an answer. He just kicked the pace up a notch until we were almost running. I was glad because the wolf was far enough ahead that her thoughts were almost gone.

We kept up that pace for a long time. How long I didn't know, just that every time the trail branched, we followed the creek bed and that was always the right choice. Sooner or later, we'd always see paw prints.

Until the dark lessened. "There's light ahead. I think we're coming to the end of the cave."

"Whatever it is, it can't be daylight. It's night out. Must be close to midnight by now. So it's got to be artificial light."

But it wasn't. The closer we got to the source of the light, the clearer it became to both of us that it was natural. Then we burst out of the cave and into a valley that stretched in front of us as far as we could see, with the dry creek bed etching a trough as it rose up a hill to our right. I followed it with my eyes until it disappeared in the forest. The origin of the creek?

Buck's thoughts took a different tack. "This is crazy. It can't be daytime. We didn't run all night."

"I know it can't be, but it is." I looked around, ignoring the dry creek bed in favor of everything else in this place that shouldn't exist but did.

"This isn't the island." We were surrounded by too many miles of wilderness. As I looked it over, I shivered. It had the look and feel of a wilderness beyond anything I'd known, though I couldn't put my finger on just what gave me that idea. But something about it was so unexpected, so totally wild, that shivers moved along my spine as I tried to come to grips with the other end of the cave.

"Lake of The Woods is huge. It took forever to reach the island and, even if the cave did go beneath the lake, we couldn't have gone far enough to be on shore now." Buck, too, inspected everything for a long, long time, turning his head one way and then another. Then, in a low voice, he said, "Dorothy, I think we're not in Kansas anymore."

"Then where are we?"

He sat down on a rock a little too quickly. "All I know is that this is where those huge wolves come from that people kept talking about. The wolves of the legends. And I also know that those wolves don't exist in our world."

"Don't be silly. We aren't in some other dimension."

He moved a hand in a small gesture. "There's no other explanation for this place." He moved closer as if needing to be close to someone. I felt the same and was glad for his shoulder touching suddenly mine, warm and solid and totally male. A part of the world I knew. "And I think I'm very glad that we didn't emerge from that cave at the wolves' den. Because I think it would have been a very bad thing if we had."

"Not bad at all." I wished the wolves were there so the silver wolf could tell me what was going on. Could prove to Buck that she wasn't dangerous. The wolf who'd briefly visited our world.

Our world.

I was already thinking in terms of two worlds.

Buck was right. We were no longer in the world we knew. I didn't know where we were, I couldn't imagine *what* this place was, let alone *where* it was. But it wasn't home.

At that moment, a stag appeared half-way up the hill, beside the dry creek bed. It paused, turned its head several times and sniffed the air. It saw us and went statue still. We, too, stopped moving. For a good five minutes, we stared at each other. Then the stag gave a quick shake of its head and disappeared in one quick bound across the creek bed and into the trees.

"There are no stags like that in Minnesota." I whispered. It seemed appropriate to whisper in this world. Wherever this world was.

"There are stags in England, but not that large."

"Perhaps everything here is larger."

"Then I hope there aren't mountain lions in this place." Buck licked his lips. "And, talking about wolves and mountain lions and any other kinds of animals that might want to eat us, I suggest we turn around and head right back to where we came from and that we don't stop until we're back at the boat and I further suggest that when we are on board, we leave. Even though in our world it's the middle of the night. And I strongly suggest we do that right now. Immediately." He held up a hand. "And know that I say that as a person who knows about wolves, dangerous predators, and what they can do. How they can tear prey to pieces."

I ignored him and pointed. "Look!"

"Where? What?" He held the flashlight like a weapon as he turned his head wildly first one way then another to see what new danger was presenting itself. "What do you see? Will it eat us?"

"I doubt it."

An eagle swooped low enough for us to see the shine of its eyes. Then lower, thrusting its legs in front of it in order to pick something up off the ground. It then flew high into the air, going straight as a string to a tall evergreen that jutted over an outcropping of the hill where the stag had disappeared. "If the eagle couldn't eat the stag, then I doubt it could eat us."

Buck sighed in relief. "I was afraid you saw a mountain lion. Or an African lion. Or worse. Because who knows what kind of animals are here?"

"We're not in Oz, Buck. I don't know where this place is but it's got to be Minnesota because that's where we were when we started." I looked judiciously about. "With a few differences."

He took a deep breath and spoke slowly, as if to a

child. "Again, and I can't emphasize this enough, we should get out of here and not return until an armed Army unit comes with us along with a few experts who I'm sure would love to know about this place."

I sat down and clasped my hands around my knees and refused to budge. He inspected me warily. "Please?"

"You do what you want. As for me, I'm not going. Not yet, anyway."

Not until the wolf returned and we got acquainted, and, hopefully, sorted out what was happening between us, though in some corner of my mind I wondered if that would happen. Miracles can't always be explained. But I wanted to try. And to do that, I had to stick around long enough to see my friend again. And she was my friend. We'd only communicated for seconds but I knew that about us. We were friends.

"I can't do that. I'll never find my way back without you. I don't have a clue how you got us here." Buck sat beside me. "Speaking of 'here', I'm thirsty. That was a long run." After a long silence, he added in a voice that said he was resigned to staying for a while at least, "Do you suppose there's any water in this strange world?"

I lifted my head in the air. Sniffed. And pointed. "Over there I think."

He looked at me as if I had two heads. "How do you know?"

I laughed. This was a strange world, but water is universal. "Buck, I come from a farm family. Smelling water is a farmer thing. I'll bet every farmer in the Midwest can do the same thing. And I smell water over there." I pointed. "It's on the wind. Can't you smell it?"

He took a few deep breaths. "Maybe, a bit, but I'm not sure and I'd never have noticed it on my own." He looked longingly in the right direction. "I hope you're right. I really am thirsty. If there aren't lions or tigers or bears between us and the water."

If we were going to stay in this place long enough to find the wolves, we'd need water. So I rose in one motion and started off, hoping I was right and that we'd find water soon. It could have been a coming rain that I smelled on the air, though, from the look of the landscape, the drought that plagued our world was just as bad in this strange place. No rain clouds anywhere. So I most likely smelled a pond or lake.

As soon as I stood up and could see a wider landscape, my fears eased and I knew we'd found water. "Weeping willows."

"They live near water."

We both ran, except we were so stiff from our earlier exertions that we slowed almost immediately and covered the remaining distance in what amounted to an extremely slow jog.

I was only then aware that my throat was parched. Still, Buck's fear of lions and tigers and bears kept me from going straight to the small pond beyond the willows. In a drought year every animal would come there looking for water. Including lions and tigers and bears if they inhabited this world.

So we both slowed as we came beneath the

weeping willows, hiding behind the long, trailing leaves until we were certain no dangerous animals were nearby. A brown rabbit the size of a dog was beside the pond along with a red squirrel that resembled those we knew, but there were no other animals in sight. So we cautiously approached the edge of the pond and then lay flat on our bellies, where we stuck our heads in the water and sated our thirst.

The water was clean and ice cold, which explained why the pond existed in a drought year. A spring was somewhere deep below ground. I judged it to be an artesian spring from the cold temperature and the force of the upwelling water that I could feel even where we lay on the edge of the pond. My family would give a year's profits from the farm for such a spring on our property.

Satisfied at last, Buck rolled over and examined the sky. "I wonder if we'll see the same constellations here as at home." His brows knitted and he rolled on one side and examined me with the same intensity he'd just given the sky. "Not that we'll know because, by the time night comes here, we'll be long gone. And safe."

"You can go if you wish. I'm staying."

He curled upwards into a sitting position and stared down at me. His eyes were the same blue as the sky behind him and his hair matched the parched world beyond. But the worried expression was his own. "You thought this trip was a wild goose chase. The only reason you came was because your brothers got sick."

"And for the money." I met his stare. "For tuition. I'm a student at Weatherby College."

He flushed. "I didn't know."

"A senior."

"Not in wolf studies. I'd know you if you were at the center."

"Medical technology. The kind of degree that'll get me a real job."

He flushed deeper. "Wolf studies isn't the most rewarding field, financially speaking. But it's my choice."

"You study a skilled predator."

"There's more to wolves than killing."

"That's the part I know."

"Then why did you come? More to the point, why'd you come after that huge wolf? You could have stayed in camp when the wolf came through and that would have been the end of it. We'd have tried to find tracks in the morning, but we'd have failed and you know it. So why are we here? And why do you refuse to return home?"

I lapsed into silence. Then, because I couldn't think of anything else to say that he'd believe, I decided to tell him part of the truth. "This wolf is different. Special."

"How, other than that it's huge?"

I licked my lips and looked away, wondering what he'd do if I told him the truth. Get as far from me as possible? Head for the cave and try to return home even if it meant getting lost and wandering about until he died alone? "I want to get to know her." His eyes flared. He knew I was telling him the truth. At last. "And I want to meet her pups. She has three."

"Three pups?" His head angled slightly, his nostrils flared. "How do you know that?"

"She told me."

He said nothing. We stared at one another for a long time. Might have stared forever were it not for a sound on the other side of the pond. On hearing it, we broke eye contact and looked across the water.

There, staring back at us was the silver wolf we'd followed through the cave.

Chapter Four

'*Y*ou came.' Her head raised, our gazes met. Her tail waved slightly. '*I'm glad you came. This thing between us, it's strange.*' She sent her thought to me. Not words, not even unspoken words and not mental pictures. Instead of any of those things, I received an idea.

I sent a thought back to her. '*I came because I want to learn more.*'

We stared at one another. This was her home, I was a visitor. I should be polite. '*Are the pups okay?*'

Her response contained relief and a touch of humor that was directed at herself. '*They are fine. As usual. I always worry when I'm gone and there's never a reason for my concern.*'

I searched the area. '*I don't see the pups.*'

'*Not now. Not yet.*' She was keeping them safe until she knew me better. Or until she knew Buck better. He was with me. Even if the silver wolf trusted me because our minds were connected she didn't know Buck. So she was careful. And she stayed on the other side of the pond.

Not so the rest of the pack. A low growl tore my mind away from the silver wolf on the other side of the water. I looked towards the sound and discovered that six wolves surrounded us and, though none quite matched the silver one in size, they were each well over two hundred pounds.

Buck moved still closer to me and hefted the flashlight like a club as if it could protect us. "Move slowly towards the cave entrance. Maybe if we can get that far they won't follow." His free hand clasped mine so tightly the circulation was cut. "But don't turn or they'll see it as cowardice and attack. Instead, back slowly." He took one step backwards, pulling me after him.

"No."

"Come on, Jane. We can survive this." Though his voice didn't sound hopeful.

I held my ground and sent my thoughts to the silver wolf across the pond. *"Please don't attack us. We won't hurt any of you or your pups."*

Her thought came back. *"They aren't angry. They are hungry."* We were food.

Would she let her pack attack? Could she stop them? I thought she could. I thought she was the alpha female. But I wasn't sure. And if she was, would she care whether we lived or died?

She barked, a high, sharp sound. The pack stopped. Milled about. Circled us several times without coming closer. And, as they milled about uncertainly, the silver wolf trotted around the pond and joined them. Came closer until mere feet separated the two of us and we stared at each other, not communicating mentally this time. Instead, we measured each other physically.

I saw a magnificent animal. I revised my estimate of her size upwards. I guessed she weighed over three hundred pounds. She was healthy, in the prime of life, with rippling muscles and silver fur that waved and gleamed until it resembled the ripples in the pond behind her. Like the water in that pond, her fur reflected the sun's rays, moving as she moved, taking the light and sending it everywhere. Her eyes were yellow and intelligent. All in all, she bore herself like the queen she was.

I had no idea what she saw when she looked at me. My heart sank as I mentally compared the two of us. Then she smiled. Yes, her lips drew back and she smiled, then she lifted her head and made a sound that could have been laughter. *"What are you? I've never seen an animal like you. Are you the only ones of your kind?"*

"We are people. There are many of us where we come from. Are there no people here in your world?"

"I don't think so."

The rest of the pack was looking to her for guidance while Buck was watching me, knowing something was going on without knowing what. His hand still held mine with a death grip and he still leaned towards the cave entrance. But he no longer tried to go there. Instead he waited.

"I'll tell the pack that you're a friend and that they should leave you alone."

The silver wolf ... I already thought of her as Silver ... moved among the other wolves, nipping and growling low until they moved back, far enough away that Buck relaxed his grip and I could let go of his hand. I shook it to restore circulation and somewhere in the back of my mind I felt shame for thinking of Buck as a distant, uncaring college professor instead of the man he obviously was.

He turned to me, wonder in his voice. "She likes you. The alpha female considers you a friend."

"I told you we talked but you didn't believe me."

"Of course I didn't. Because it's impossible. But you two definitely have something going on." Amazement gave his voice a lilt I'd not heard before.

"Something, yes."

"Which means you knew there were wolves on the island all along." The lilt turned into an accusation. "You lied when you said there weren't any."

"I didn't know about the wolves. Truly, I didn't. The first time I knew was when she came through our campsite." But he was right about one thing. Nothing about our situation made sense. "We communicate. Somehow."

"Telepathically?" He snorted his disbelief.

"Maybe."

"That's crap."

"I don't know how we communicate, I just know that we do." I turned towards him. "Buck, it's no harder to believe in telepathy than it is to believe that this place exists." I waved an arm to take in the whole of the world around us.

He raked a hand through his hair until it resembled spiky straw. "Both things are impossible, I'll give you that."

He began to believe. I could see it in his eyes as he took a step away from me, away from the cave entrance and towards the wolves.

That step was a mistake. Before his foot touched the ground, six huge wolves formed a circle around him. One movement and he'd be dead. He stopped breathing, we both did, and that foot touched the earth only enough to give him balance. He didn't shift his weight at all.

"He's my friend. He likes wolves even more than I do. Please don't let anyone hurt him." I said the words out loud as I said them in my mind, but I didn't realize it until I saw Buck's startled look towards me.

Silver went into action. Silently, low to the ground and moving like a ghost, she went among the pack, nosing them, pushing them gently aside, letting them know Buck was not to be harmed any more than I was. The wolves backed off until they were far enough away to sit on their haunches and stare at the two of us.

We were intruders in their world but friends of their alpha female. If Silver wanted them to leave us alone, they wouldn't touch a hair of our heads. Somehow I knew that.

"Thank you," Buck said in a voice that wasn't quite under control as he finally stood with two feet planted firmly on the ground. And stared at Silver as he'd stare at a ghost, mouth open, fear and awe chasing each other across his face. "I believe you. And now I don't want to go home." He moved, looking at Silver and then at the other wolves. "Because this is amazing. The wolves are amazing. As long as she's around to keep them in line."

I asked Silver if the wolves would hurt us when she was gone. *"Of course not."*

"They won't bother us. Silver promised."

Buck sat on a rock. Looked around. Was glad the wolves stayed back, though I wished they'd come closer so we could get acquainted. Took a deep breath. "So now what?"

I looked around too. "I don't know. I want to visit with Silver, get to know her and her pups. See if I can come again when there's another drought."

"What's the drought got to do with it?" Then he hit his head. "Of course. If the creek was at its normal depth, no one could get through the cave. The door between worlds, if that's what the cave is, wouldn't be open."

"The water level must have been low enough during other years for the wolves to come across. That's where the legends came from. But only in drought years and then, when they got through the cave, they were unable to get off the island. So no one ever learned about them."

"If it rains, the cave will fill and we won't get home."

I looked at the sky. "No clouds in sight."

"If we see clouds, we run through that cave as fast as possible. I don't want to be stuck here forever."

"Until then, we can get acquainted with the wolves."

A small smile began on Buck's face. Then spread

until his whole face beamed. "A new type of wolf. Dire wolves, perhaps, trapped here for thousands of years by high water in the cave."

"We can't tell anyone about them. Or anything about this world, whatever it is. Wherever it is."

"We can and we will." He looked about and relented a bit. "These wolves will make my career."

"No!" I didn't know I shouted until he backed a bit and the wolves, still yards away, rose from their haunches and moved closer. Watched Buck, ears flat, growls coming from their throats. Circled him and, in doing so, circled me, too.

Buck thought we were about to be attacked. He put his arms around me in a protective gesture. The quintessential male. I appreciated that he would save me if he could but I wasn't the one needing protection from the huge animals now close enough that I could smell them. A feral scent of earth and trees and wild places.

Buck was the one in danger because of my reaction to his statement. I'd not allow him to turn my new friend into a research subject but neither could I let him die.

I waved at the wolves to let them know I wasn't angry. I shushed them, and they backed off, looking from me to Silver and back. She watched and did nothing but some signal must have passed among them because one of the wolves whimpered a bit, cocking its head and looking hard at me.

I took Buck's hand in mine and pulled him closer. Then I turned to the wolves to reinforce Silver's command to leave us alone. "See, guys. This is Buck. He's my friend. He's a good guy." I glared at Buck but kept a smile on my face for the sake of the wolves. "Most of the time."

They relented and left us alone. One of them, a light gray male of about two hundred pounds curled up on the grass and closed its eyes for a snooze. The rest milled about then found other things to do. One left, heading back to the thicket they'd come from. Because the pups were there?

"They are safe there." Unsaid was that Silver didn't trust our new psychic connection enough to allow access to her pups. Or she didn't trust Buck.

Buck coughed. It didn't startle the wolves, they got sick too and recognized the sound. But I went into overdrive. "You're still sick."

"A cold. No big deal." But his arms dropped to his sides and he slumped somewhat. "But I will admit that I'm tired. I thought I was over it after resting all day yesterday, but that trip through the cave was tiring. I could sleep for a month." He looked glumly about. "If there was a bed handy."

I looked too, my gaze finally settling on a nearby patch of grass so tall that if either of us walked into it, we'd disappear in two steps. "I'll bet that grass is soft." I moved away slowly, checking the wolves to make sure they didn't attack Buck as soon as we were apart. But the pack had got the message and they ignored him, though they followed me with interest. What was this strange friend of Silver's up to now?

I waded into the tall grass and yanked an armful

out by the roots and lay them on the ground, in the intense sun. I bowed to Buck, indicating he lay down. "I'll have a nice bed in no time."

"I can't sleep there." He turned, making a complete circle. "Not anywhere in this world. What I was trying to say in my clumsy way was that it's time to go home." He coughed again.

He wanted to go so he could return with a large contingent of people and equipment. Cameras, syringes for blood samples, tranquillizer darts. But Silver was my friend now. Friends look out for each other. I couldn't allow the pack to be turned into lab animals. "It's like you said, it's a long trip back through the cave. A nap is in order. When you're rested, we'll talk about going home." And a few other things. Like keeping secrets.

He eyed the grass bed greedily. "I suppose a short nap wouldn't hurt."

"You're sick. Sick people should nap often."

He gave in and eased his large frame onto the grass bed while I gathered more that I added to the pile as he rolled from side to side to allow me to shove them beneath him. He wiggled his shoulders. "It is comfortable."

"You shouldn't be surprised. I know my way around the forest."

"I thought I did too but I've never slept on grass before." He fingered the long blades in a kind of wonder. "It's not even scratchy."

His comment made me examine the grass I held closely. "It sort of resembles the smooth brome that grows everywhere back home, but it's taller, seven feet and more, and the blades are feathery and soft." Perfect material for a mattress. "I'm a farmer's daughter. I can spot a noxious weed from a thousand feet and this isn't one." I shrugged. "But it does have me stumped."

He gazed at me, and then at the entire new world we were in. "I'm sure it is what you called it. Smooth brome. But in this world, it's different. Changed. Because it evolved differently. Like the wolves."

A reminder that we were in another world, another universe, one that couldn't exist but did. "I wonder what else is different. Changed. Similar to what we know but not quite the same." His sharp glance in the direction of the wolves told me what difference was important to him. Wolves, not grass. Then turning his face to the sun and spreading his arms and legs the better to let his body absorb its heat he simply closed his eyes and fell asleep.

He coughed in his sleep. I'm not good about illness, I hardly ever get sick, but it seemed to me that the cough was different than it had been earlier. Tighter. Sicker. I wished I knew what pneumonia sounded like. I was afraid that might be what his cold was turning into. I hated that I didn't know and decided that as soon as he awoke, we'd go back through the cave because I couldn't take a chance on his health.

I'd get him to a doctor as soon as he gave his solemn promise not to reveal the existence of the wolves. Not to anyone. Not ever. Even if it meant spending the rest of his life as an assistant professor instead of a world famous full professor of wolf studies.

As the hours passed and he slept as if drugged, I decided that time in this world must be different from time back home. I had no way of telling time, but I was sure that more hours were passing without night coming than I was used to. Not to mention that the events of the past hours were getting to me and I couldn't process anything, not even time.

When Buck finally awoke the sun was still high in the sky but he was as refreshed as if he'd slept the night through. So he was either not as sick as I'd thought or time in this world was skewed.

He sat up and stretched. "I feel like a new man." So much for pneumonia and maybe we didn't have to leave so soon after all. He rose in one smooth motion, the movement of a healthy male, and joined me. "Okay."

"What's okay? What are you talking about?"

"You were right." His arms lifted to the sun, drinking in its heat. "I was tired, which is a whole different thing than being sick. I'm now rested, and I agree with you that we should stick around and learn more about these wolves."

I was suspicious. "I still don't want anyone told about them."

He thought that over and nodded slowly. Sighed. "Okay. I can see your point. They aren't circus animals. But I want to get to know them for myself, not so I can become famous. They are unique animals. Wolves that haven't existed in our world for thousands of years. Maybe never. They are wonderful. Beautiful."

He could be lying. I'd not know the difference. My brothers lied all the time when we were kids and I fell for their lies every time. Once they said there was a rattlesnake in the back yard that was out to bite me and, even though there are no rattlesnakes in the area I wouldn't go outside. Another time they said an ice cream truck was coming and they'd get me a cone if I gave them money, even though no truck selling ice cream or any other kind of treat ever made it to our remote farm. I believed them that time too and lost my allowance and my parents said I should have known better than to believe them.

So I learned about lies and now I stared at Buck through lowered eyelids and crossed my arms in front of me. No way would I show him the way home until I believed his motive was pure. "Before you wanted to bring an army. Why the change of plans?"

He came close. So close my breathing stopped though I could hear his breath, see the trees behind me reflected in his eyes and count the tiny wrinkles around them. Not age, he wasn't old enough for wrinkles, so he must be outside a lot. "That little nap helped more than I expected. I feel fine. I don't need a doctor."

He took a deep breath. "I want to stick around and get to know them. To learn." He leaned over to stick his face in mine. "At least I can do that. I study wolves because I find them fascinating, not because I want to become famous." He pulled himself back to his original posture. "Though fame and fortune would be nice." His voice was so forlorn that I believed him at last.

Maybe I was being suckered but I wanted to trust him. "Good."

He crossed his arms and gave me a searching look. "So now what? You're the expert. An outdoors person more than I am." He unfolded his arms and spread them wide. "What do we do now?"

His chin pointed to the sun that had finally, finally begun a downwards descent towards night. "How do we get through the coming night? More to the point, what do we eat? Or don't we?" He rubbed his stomach to emphasize his words. A hard stomach, he didn't spend all his hours in an office grading papers.

He'd asked good questions. I bit my lip and considered them one at a time. "We gather more grass for a bigger bed. One large enough for two people. As to food, I don't know." I cast a look around. "Berries, maybe?"

"How do we know they won't be poisonous?"

I bit my lip again. "We don't. But if we don't want to starve to death, we might look for berries that resemble the ones we know from our world."

"And hope they didn't evolve into poison?"

"What choice do we have?"

"We are going hunting." The thought was clear. *"We'll find something. Not much, rabbits, most likely because it's late and no large animals are nearby. We'll share."*

She had heard my thought. "The pack will share their kill. A rabbit most likely."

"There's a thicket nearby. It's crawling with rabbits." A place where rabbits could usually hide from predators. *"Often one or more of them strays into an open area and we get them. Rabbits don't keep the pack well fed, but they'll do until we can go on a real hunt."*

A picture of the island came from her mind. She'd been scouting the island as a place to find large game. *"No large animals there."*

"So I discovered."

Buck's shoulders hunched and his face changed. "I'd almost forgotten that you can talk to the alpha female."

"Silver. Her name is Silver."

"So they give us a rabbit. How do we cook it? Or do we eat it raw?" His voice said he'd rather starve than eat raw meat.

We were in an area of boulders, both large and small. And I had matches in my pocket. "We can cook them."

"There's a drought and we forgot to bring a stove. If a campfire would start a forest fire back on the island, won't it do the same here?"

I walked a few yards and kicked a couple rocks. "We can make a ring of rocks beside the pond on the sand where there's no grass to catch fire. We can limit the wood we use to kinds that don't flare or send many sparks. Oak, if we can find it. Before we start the fire, we lay a large rock in the center and put the meat on it. As the fire heats the rock, the meat will cook."

Surprise covered his face. "It just might work."

"I've never done it, but my Brownie leader said it would work if any of us was ever lost in the woods and hungry and had matches and a small, dead animal available."

The wolves disappeared. No words, no thought, nothing that I could see but suddenly they all went alert and slipped into the forest. Knowing what they'd be doing, we set about finding stones.

We found enough large stones to cage a campfire plus an additional larger one with a depression in the center that we could use for cooking. "We could make soup in that depression." I remembered what Silver had said. That rabbits weren't large enough game to keep the pack well fed. Taking their much-needed meat might be wrong. "Soup is a good idea if we can find some vegetables so we won't need much meat."

"What aren't you telling me?"

"That they are getting hungry. That they'll need to go on a hunt soon for something large."

"Us?" His eyes went wide, and his breath stopped.

"Of course not us. We're accepted. We're part of the pack so they won't hurt us. But they need to kill something, and soon."

"I'm beginning to see wolves in a whole new way."

"As predators?"

"As you've seen them all along. And these wolves are larger than either of us."

"They won't hurt us, I told you that."

"But they could, with one snap of their jaws, one slice of their teeth."

He was right. It could happen. Which meant we

shouldn't stay in this other world too long. Silver was my friend and she was the alpha female, the leader of the pack. She wouldn't let any wolf hurt us. But what if she was gone for a while? Or was hurt and could no longer lead? What then?

I pushed the thought away and turned to more immediate concerns. "Now to find some vegetables."

Buck put his hands on his hips. "Where do we start looking?"

There was a swampy side to the pond. "Over there. Cattails."

"We eat cattails?"

"The roots. Then we'll look for berries or leafy greens."

Buck gulped a couple times and then followed me to the swamp where we dug some cattails with our bare hands. It wasn't hard. The swamp was drying out but the part with the cattails was still soft mud.

Berries were a different story. Wandering through a nearby field we found some that resembled strawberries, and more that we thought were blueberries. "Wrong seasons. They shouldn't be ripe at the same time. But they look like berries from our world."

"So what do we do?" Buck inspected the berries in his hand. "Eat some and hope we don't die?"

"Do you have a better idea?" He shook his head and sighed. Then carefully chose the smallest strawberry and ate it.

But when he started to do the same with a blueberry, I stopped him. "I'll try the blueberry. That way, if one of us gets sick, we'll know which kind of berry to avoid."

He nodded agreement. We gathered a few more berries but our enthusiasm waned as we waited to see if we'd topple over and die. We found a boulder and sat in the sun and twisted dry grasses into strings that we'd use as kindling to get our fire started. And we waited for stomach aches that never came.

By the time the sun was almost touching the horizon, we'd decided the berries were, indeed, similar to the ones in our world and were edible. We decided to take a chance on the cattail roots as there was no third person in our party to test them on.

The fire started easily. When the wolves returned, shock and fear was easy to see in their eyes. "Wild animals are afraid of fire." I started towards the wolves.

"For good reason." Buck stayed between the wolves and the fire.

I sent a thought to Silver. *'We control the fire. We need it to prepare food before eating it. You'll be safe. We won't let the fire spread beyond the ring of rocks on the sand.'*

She kept herself between the rest of the pack and the two of us on the sand. The protector of her family. *"If you say so."* She was making a huge leap of faith in trusting me. But she was cautious.

I took the meat she offered, pulled it to pieces and kept just a small portion, then gave the rest back to her. *"This will be enough for us and your pups must be hungry."*

"That's not enough to keep you both alive."

"We also eat plants so we don't need so much meat."

That information surprised her. But she took back the extra meat and took it around the pond where she disappeared into the thicket on the other side. So rabbits weren't the only animals that were safe in prickly brush. Wolf pups could also stay there.

Silver didn't retur,n and I noticed that Black, the large wolf whom I took to be her mate, also disappeared into the thicket. Which left the rest of the pack, five large wolves of various shades of black and gray, to watch as we cooked dinner on the rock in the center of the fire, a stew of some kind of meat neither of us recognized, cattail roots as a substitute for potatoes, and berries instead of carrots.

It tasted wonderful or else we were so hungry we didn't care. We took turns using Buck's aluminum cup as a bowl. It had been dangling from his belt when we ran pell-mell from our camp after Silver and into another world and having it now made life much easier.

The wolves watched from a safe distance, nervous and anxious, pacing back and forth until we finished eating and put out the fire. Only then did they relax. Two of them came closer, though not close enough to touch. They sat on their haunches and inspected us.

No true bed awaited us, just grass to make the ground softer and as the sun dropped behind the horizon, a chill settled on the landscape. Buck started coughing again, that tight cough that could mean nothing or that could be pneumonia. Will had had pneumonia once, and Buck's cough sounded a lot like Will's had.

"We maybe should leave in the morning." I wished it was still light so I could see him better. See how sick he was. We'd agreed to use the flashlight only in emergencies in order to save the batteries.

"Or we could stay a few days and study the wolves."

"You're the one who wanted to leave."

His shoulders hunched. "That was before. Because I know how dangerous wolves can be. But do you realize what's happening? A wolf and a human have a psychic link. You can learn from your friend and I can learn more about wolves in a day than I could in a year anywhere else."

"But you can't tell anyone." Panic curled through my innards.

"I won't have to. I'll know how they think. When we return to our world, I'll better understand the wolves at the center. No one will have to know where I learned so much."

He seemed sincere. "A couple days, then. That'll finish out the week of the original contract with my brothers."

Our glances met and Buck's eyebrows shot up. "Though how we'll know when a week has passed is beyond me. Time here is different."

"If I don't return home on time, my brothers will come looking. When they don't find us, they'll turn the island upside down and find the cave."

"Two days, then. No more."

I nodded agreement. He started to do the same but coughed instead. He hugged his arms around his middle to try and keep warm. "The grass won't make a decent blanket. The wind will blow it off." My words were barely out before he dropped into the bed of grass, snuggling deeply and failing to pull it over him. I followed and soon wished for a blanket as the night turned dark and cooled considerably. But we had none.

Buck's cough grew worse as the hours passed. I couldn't sleep for worrying about him. I passed the time studying stars that were not the familiar ones of our world. A shiver went through me at this added proof that we were in another world. Another universe.

I moved closer to Buck and wrapped my arms around him, willing my body heat to warm him, hoping his would do the same to me. But he was cold. So cold.

A movement at the edge of my vision caught my attention. One of the wolves was coming near, a black form in a black night. Then another. And another. My breath stopped. I waited to be torn apart because in the dark they could do as they wished without Silver knowing.

Instead, the first wolf dropped to the ground beside me, snuggling close and wrapping itself around my body. A second did the same for Buck. The third lay at our feet. None of them made a sound. They simply closed their eyes and went back to sleep. But we were now warm, enclosed in a cocoon of thick fur that was better than any blanket could possibly be. Buck's cough slowed and then stopped. And we slept that way, warm and safe, until the sun came up in the morning.

Chapter Five

When I awoke I found myself eye to eye with a large, medium gray wolf. It was inches away and watching me with a curiosity that equaled mine but with none of my trepidation. Having spent the night wrapped in the warmth of the wolf's fur, I wasn't afraid, but I was cautious. "Hi." I made no sudden move, just in case it wasn't as friendly as it looked.

A tail wag was my answer and ears cocked forward.

"My name's Jane. What's yours?"

Another wag as it scooted a bit closer still.

"If I get up, will you eat me?" A snort from Buck said he'd heard the conversation. I defended my remark. "I think they are friendly but I'm not stupid."

"We'd already be eaten and digested if that was their intent." He moved, stretched, and raised himself on one elbow until he was looking down on me, and, incidentally, at the wolves surrounding us. But he moved carefully, slowly so he wasn't as carefree as he pretended. Besides, he knew a lot about wolves. "There's another wolf a few yards away. It's already up and ready for the day."

"Maybe these guys are sticking close to keep us

warm. We should get up so they can get going too."

Buck had blue eyes. Had I noticed before? I couldn't remember. In the bright light of morning, he seemed new and unknown. Taller, broader, stronger. More intelligent. Nicer, even though he did have a cold. Hopefully it was just a cold, nothing truly bad.

I hoped not to regret agreeing to stay a couple of days. Buck could learn about wolves and I could advance my friendship with Silver, but not if Buck was truly sick. I reached out to touch him, to feel his forehead, but he moved out of range before my hand reached his forehead and he acted okay.

I wondered where Silver was. I didn't see her and decided to try an experiment to see how strong our psychic connection was. To find out if we had to be in sight of one another for it to work. I sent out a thought. *"Where are you? Are you okay?"*

The answer came back almost immediately. *"I'm with the pups."*

"I hope they are okay."

A mental chuckle, a motherly thing. *"They are fine."* Then a stray thought, not meant for me but I heard it. *"They are old enough to leave the den. To start learning about the world."* Followed by a thought that was directed towards me. *"Want to meet them?"*

"I'd love to meet your family."

Another chuckle. *"You've already met most of my family. Three of them kept you warm last night."*

"It was chilly. Tell them thanks."

A mental nod. *"I'll do that but they know."* Then, *"We'll be there in a bit."*

Buck was watching me closely. "You're talking with that wolf again, aren't you?"

"She's coming soon with the pups." My stomach growled. "And I'm glad because I'm hungry. I hope breakfast will be soon."

Buck leaned back on his elbows and examined me. "I guess you don't know as much about wolves as you thought you did."

"What do you mean?"

"Don't expect them to bring breakfast. Wolves don't eat three meals a day. Not even one meal every day. Once or twice a week or less."

I doubled over. "Oh dear."

"Good thing there are berries nearby."

"We'd better get busy and find some." A movement across the pond, from the thicket, caught my attention. "After we meet the kids."

There were three of them. One was black and one was medium gray, but the third, the smallest, was as white as snow. "They are beautiful."

Silver must have heard my thought as I spoke because a sly answer came into my mind. *"I think so, but I'm their mother so I might be prejudiced."*

"Boys?"

"Two boys and a girl."

"Just like me. I have two brothers."

The white pup trailed her brothers. Something about her made me look closer. She had a limp. It was slight but it was there. I couldn't hide my shock from Silver, who replied, *"I know."*

I saw a picture from her mind of the white pup

snoozing at the bottom of a hill when a rock came down. It hit a bump and flew into the air and landed on the pup's foreleg. The pup cried out and couldn't walk for a long time. *"I was concerned until she got better. But the leg isn't yet right. She's still slower than her brothers."* I knew that in the wolf world being slow could mean being left behind. It could mean being dead but, with effort, I hid that thought from Silver.

Instead, I simply said, *"I'm so sorry."*

"I'm sure she'll be fine in time. Until then, the pack will care for her." But there was concern in Silver's thoughts though she tried to shove it aside. She was the pack leader and she couldn't dwell on one member, even if that member was her own daughter. *"She has eyes like yours."*

"Blue. I have blue eyes."

"You two are like my children in that way."

"I'd love to have a little sister."

Buck saw the pup's limp. "The wolf world is brutal."

"Shh! She'll hear you."

He looked at me as if I'd gone mad. "I don't share the same mind link you two do, and I doubt she understands English."

I was about to shush him again when Silver and the pups reached us and we were drowned in a mass of puppies. Behind them was the black male I'd figured was Silver's mate. Almost as large as Silver and with the same patrician carriage, he was a fitting consort.

We sat on the ground and got to know the pups. "Hi, kids."

Buck loved them. Held them. Cuddled them as they crawled all over us and we examined them. The two males were identical except that one was a darker gray than the other. The female, however, held my attention.

"She must be an albino. There aren't any other white wolves in the pack."

Buck took her from my arms. Silver watched his every move but didn't interrupt. "Not a true albino. Her eyes are blue, they'd be pink if she was a complete albino." He examined the skin closely. "But, yes, I believe you're right about the white colored fur being a form of albinism." He petted the pup, she leaned into him, and he cuddled her close, touching her nose. "She'll burn easily in the sun."

Silver saw Buck with her pup and approved. *"I wasn't sure about him. But he likes my daughter."*

Buck and I examined the pups more thoroughly. It was easy to differentiate the white female from the gray males. Distinguishing one gray male from the other wasn't so easy. Finally, in desperation, I said, "The dark one is Uno. The lighter is Dos."

Buck grinned. "Is that the best you can do? Number One and Number Two?"

"I'm not very imaginative."

"Then the white female is Tres?"

"Number Three." I considered her as she reached across Buck's arm to lick my wrist. "I suppose so."

My stomach growled. Buck heard. "We need to find food."

I told Silver that we'd be gone for a while. She

understood and passed the word to the rest of the pack so they wouldn't become suspicious when we left. Then Buck and I set out to explore the nearby area and see what we could find to eat besides two kinds of berries and some cattail roots.

We went past the small field where we'd found the berries before and gathered raspberries, dandelions and wild carrots in our shirts. "I'm sure there will be more if we look farther. But this will do for breakfast."

We ate the raspberries while we cooked the greens on the stone surrounded by fire. Again, the wolves stayed away, but this time not as far as before. They were learning that the fire in the ring of rocks wasn't to be feared. We had to teach the pups not to stray too close. They were fearless and eager to investigate everything. But we managed to keep them safe until breakfast was ready. Then we put out the fire and poured water over the stones to cool them so the pups couldn't burn themselves if they strayed too close. Then, at last, not knowing what time of day it was in this strange world, we ate.

"Will you watch the pups while we hunt?" Silver had been watching us play with her pups.

I remembered our fears when we first entered this other world. That was how I thought of it. As the other world. Now I made the two words one. Otherworld. *"We aren't as large as you and we don't have your teeth. If a large predator comes, we might not be able to fight it off."*

Buck's eyes narrowed. "You're talking with that

wolf again, aren't you?"

"She wants us to watch the kids while the pack hunts." I told him my concern about large animals. A muscle in his face twitched. He'd been the first to mention large animals when we first emerged from the cave. He shared my concern.

I spoke to Silver. *"I'm afraid we won't be able to protect them."*

Silver dropped to her haunches. She stared at me. *"We need every member of the pack to find food. It's dry, prey is scarce and hard to find. You have fire. Fire can burn."*

I turned to Buck, "She thinks we can protect them with fire."

His lips pursed. "We could make another campfire and have sticks nearby to set on fire and use as weapons. With fire we can protect the pups."

So I told Silver we'd babysit after we scoured the area for sticks of the right size. We found some so, when the fire was going, the pack left to look for food.

Chapter Six

We set the sticks near the fire and piled enough wood nearby to last the entire day. Then we settled down to a day of playing with pups and eating wild berries.

"A perfect time to learn about wolves." Buck lifted Tres into his lap. "I wish I had some way to draw blood. I'd love to get a sample of their DNA. Of course it'll be different from wolves in our world, but I'd like to know if it'll show a connection between these wolves and wolves in our world."

I was glad he couldn't get his wish. "I don't want proof of the existence of these wolves to follow us home. Until the river rises and seals the passage between worlds, the danger of discovery is too high to take a chance." His shrug said he didn't agree but he wouldn't argue with me.

The pups alternated playing with each other, crawling all over us, and napping as we lounged against a log we'd hauled near the fire. I found everything around us to be exciting and kept turning and twisting to see things I'd missed earlier. Birch trees with needles instead of leaves. Grass softer than down. Huge birds that resembled eagles but weren't floating on the thermals, eyes on the ground as they searched for prey. Flowers that were larger and brighter than any in my world. But then, everything in Otherworld was larger. Brighter. More colorful.

Time passed. Buck and I nibbled berries and watched the sun cross the sky, debating whether the journey towards night truly took longer in Otherworld or whether it just seemed that way. Neither of us had a watch and cell phones didn't work so we couldn't check.

"I think the time here is the same." Buck's voice was low, hardly more than a whisper as his eyelids drooped and he fought to stay awake. In the heat of the day his cough had disappeared. The hot sun was doing his body good.

"I think a day has more hours here." I looked away because his relaxation was contagious, and I didn't want to fall asleep on the job. Watching the pups was a huge responsibility. I didn't want to blow it.

As I considered how many hours there might be in a day here in Otherworld, we heard a snarl. The pups heard it before we did. One second the two males were tumbling over the ground and the female, Tres, was playing with a weed that had been dragged across the sand behind our log, and the next second all three were in our laps quaking in fear.

We sat up fast. Looked at each other, agreeing that something must be wrong though we didn't know what. Looked around and saw nothing. Wished we had the heightened senses of wolves. Grabbed sticks and dipped their tips into the fire until we held blazing torches.

Then we stood up slowly, dumping the pups into a ball at our feet, where they lay tightly curled and shivering in fear. Then we waited and watched, turning one way and then another in order to better see what was surely coming.

We didn't have long to wait. A bear lumbered out of the trees and towards us. Its eyes were on the pups. A grizzly, a monster of an animal, as large as a small truck. It reared onto its hind legs as it advanced. Pure terror immobilized me.

Buck, however, moved. I'd not have expected it of a city person, but he had learned about the wilderness while working with wolves and he walked slowly but surely towards the grizzly, waving the fire stick as he moved. He spread his arms wide. I remembered hearing somewhere that if a bear threatens, making yourself appear as large as possible might make it think twice about attacking.

Not this bear. It didn't stop.

The two drew closer until only yards separated them. Then they both stopped. The grizzly roared and pawed the air. Buck waved the fire stick and took another step towards it. The bear didn't retreat.

It was up to me. I kicked the pups close to the minimal protection of the log and joined Buck, holding my own fire stick. We waved the sticks and took baby steps towards the grizzly. It didn't come closer but it didn't retreat either.

I was terrified. I was sure it could smell my fear and was afraid that scent would lead it to overcome its fear of fire. If that happened it would be on us in seconds. We would die in this world, unknown, our bodies never found, and so would the pups.

The bear suddenly went quiet. It dropped to four legs. Swung its head back and forth, sniffing the air. And moved its attention elsewhere.

Then we heard it. Howling. Barking. The pack was back from the hunt. They'd either heard of smelled the grizzly and were coming in fast and ready for a fight. They charged the grizzly, snapping at its legs, feinting and parrying as the bear swung at them, chasing them away. But they always came back. With the pack to take attention away from us, Buck and I came closer, swinging our fire sticks. When we were close enough, Buck swung his stick at the grizzly's face.

It gave a howl and the odor of burning fur filled the air. Then, pawing the air, it turned and ran back into the trees, screaming in pain.

I returned to the fire, pushed my stick into the sand to put the fire out, and sagged to the log, where I gathered the pups into my lap and hugged them as the pack gathered around, nosing and sniffing until two went to the edge of the trees where they picked up sizable chunks of meat that they'd dropped upon seeing the bear.

The pack soon shrugged off what had happened. They calmly went about their routine, feeding the pups and giving us enough to flavor the soup they figured must be our usual fare. The incident with the bear was behind them. Buck understood better than I did. "They are used to this sort of thing. This is their life."

"It was awful. The pups could have been killed."

"But they weren't. Neither were we, thank goodness." Buck debated whether to continue, before saying, "It's the way of the world, both this world and ours unless you're safe in a house."

"Then I'm glad I live in a house." I hugged Tres closer. She was the fragile one and so tiny. "She's just a baby."

Buck came close and leaned over me. A muscle in his cheek jumped as he tried to hide that he, too, was having a hard time getting past what almost happened but he was large and solid and safe and not as afraid as I was and I wanted to stay in his shadow forever. "Cuddle her while you can. Someday she'll grow up and must take her place in the pack."

I touched Tres' leg where it had healed crooked. "She can't run as fast as the others. What will happen to her?"

I wanted him to guarantee her safety. He couldn't. "She might be okay. Wolves care for their own." But his voice said otherwise. His voice said she'd die young.

I held her tight to me until she wiggled free and went to play with her brothers. Like their elders, what had happened was already behind them. They were happy because their family was back.

At that moment, the trees shivered. Silver lay in the sun, her fur keeping her warm even as the breeze now sweeping through the forest grew and turned cool. Her eyes were heavy with satisfaction and the happiness of being with her family. But her thoughts met mine. *"Your mate. Is he a good hunter?"*

Buck? My mate? I started to laugh even as I

hugged myself to keep warm in the sudden cooling of the day. Then, even as laughter rose in my throat, I caught sight of Buck, standing in the sun with the wind ruffling his hair and billowing his shirt and, somehow, he looked different than he had only seconds earlier. Because of Silver's thoughts? Because she thought we were mates? Because her belief about us made me see him differently?

I saw him as a man. As a mate. Couldn't help it.

He'd picked up Tres and was scratching her belly as she pawed the air and greedily accepted all the attention he was willing to heap upon her. I was used to my brothers, who can wipe anyone off a bar floor, so I was used to rippling muscles and tight bodies and until now I hadn't paid over much attention to Buck's physique. Now I couldn't ignore him so I inspected him covertly under cover of watching him play with Tres.

I wondered where, growing up in a city, he'd got those muscles and the tan and sun-bleached hair that came from a lot of time spent out-of-doors. As soon as I asked myself, I knew the answer. From chasing wolves, of course.

I'd only thought of him as a college professor but he was more than that. He was a wolf researcher and his research took him into the wilderness some of the time. All that activity along with his natural endowments had turned him into a very hunky, good-looking man. I wondered how many female students took his classes just to be able to worship his physique. Probably lots.

I strolled over to where he sat on our log with Tres

in his lap. He was tickling her. She couldn't get enough of his attention. I was almost jealous. I sat beside them and reached out one hand to touch Tres and, unintentionally, my hand brushed against Buck's. The previous night I'd slept with my arms around him without my body reacting the way it did now. The difference sent a shock through me. I withdrew as if burned.

Buck looked up. "Is something wrong?"

"No. Of course not." I rose quickly and walked away. But I couldn't find any place to walk to and soon found myself strolling everywhere restlessly, unable to settle down, until I was once again beside Buck and Tres. And once again, I accidentally bumped into him. Sort of accidentally. Wanted to know if the same thing would happen again, if the same electricity would shock my system. I saw a bit of mud on his cheek. Reached out to wipe it away, feeling foolish for doing so. Touched his skin. And took a deep, shocked, breath and forgot how attractive he was in the realization that he was sicker than I'd have thought possible.

How could it have happened without me noticing? When had he developed a fever? "You're burning up."

He shrugged off my announcement. "It's a hot day."

"Not anymore." But he hadn't noticed because as the day cooled, his body grew more heated. "It's growing cooler."

Clearly annoyed, he pointed to a sun that beat down mercilessly. But it no longer had enough heat to keep us warm though I knew I couldn't convince him of that. I shivered, partly from the wind, partly from fear for this new problem in a foreign universe, but he was warm and comfortable and unconcerned.

I studied the sky, looking for a change, for something to prove to him that the weather was changing, but everything seemed the same. No clouds were gathering. The only difference was the breeze that grew stiffer as we sat on the log and the wolf pack lay around and digested their dinner. Once the black male lifted his muzzle and sniffed the air but lay down again almost immediately and closed his eyes.

I rose. "I'll get some greens and make soup with the meat the pack brought."

"If you wish." Buck leaned against our log and closed his eyes much as the black male had done. But now that I knew Buck had a fever, I could see the difference between the two males. Buck wasn't relaxing because he wasn't truly sleepy. He was sick, he just didn't know it.

"We should start for home."

He shook his head. "One more day, remember? I'm just beginning to know the pack. One more day will be priceless." He coughed and seemed irritated that something so trivial as a cold wasn't gone yet.

The chill of the changing weather was creeping from the trees and reaching out to touch us but Buck was too hot to notice. "I vote that we leave now." He should see a doctor, he might need antibiotics. I still wondered about pneumonia.

He rolled his eyes. "No way but I'll agree to leave the morning after if you're so darned eager to get back home."

"It's turning cold and you're sick."

"I'm not sick any more. I'm not coughing."

We argued. Nothing I said could convince him that he was sick or that we should leave. He slid a hand along Tres' soft, white fur. "These wolves are wonderful."

I argued that we should leave though, in his fevered state, he didn't listen. We argued for a long time and eventually found ourselves standing, squared off and staring at one another.

Then it began to rain.

While we'd argued, clouds had formed and we'd not noticed. Not huge, dark clouds, but I could see ones that were large and black and towering coming on the horizon, flying swiftly across the sky towards us. Bad weather was reaching out with its fingers to grab us. A downpour was in the black clouds that were coming fast.

Then they came and I held out a hand and let it fill with raindrops. "It's raining. The creek will fill, the cave will be blocked. We have to leave while we still can. Soon. Now." I made a slight movement towards the cave, hoping he'd follow. We'd arrived with nothing, we had nothing to pack. We could simply walk into the cave and return home.

He didn't follow. Instead he lifted his face to the rain and smiled and that was when I understood how bad his fever was. His eyes glittered as eyes do when someone is delirious, but I didn't realize how bad off he was until he said his next words. "The rain is cool. It feels so good."

He turned his face to the sky the better to feel the water on his face and smiled as if he was in complete control of his faculties. "It's not raining hard." No it wasn't, but those dark clouds were tumbling over one another. A terrible storm was coming fast. I watched in concern as they boiled over us but Buck either didn't notice or, in his delirium, didn't care. "We should stay today. I promise we'll leave tomorrow."

I took another step towards the cave, watching Buck closely, hoping he'd come, but he didn't move. Frustrated, I retraced my steps, took his arm and tugged gently. "Buck, come. We have to go."

Chapter Seven

For a moment I thought it would work. He let me lead him up the hill towards the cave. Half a dozen more steps and we'd be on our way. But it didn't happen. "What are you trying to do?" He grew angry. "I'm not leaving." He shook my hand away and turned back to the wolves.

He didn't see the rock in his path so he couldn't stop himself from falling over it and sliding down the hill on the newly wet grass, rolling and tumbling. It wasn't a long fall, it wasn't a high hill. But he landed in a jackknifed position, one arm between another boulder and his body. His sharp shout of pain said something was wrong.

I ran to him. He pulled himself upright and tried to bring the arm that had been pinned around to check it. What we both saw made me stop breathing. "It's broken." No bone stuck out, thank goodness, but the odd angle of his arm said without doubt that he had a broken arm.

The pain brought him out of his delirium as no argument had. "We have to get out of here." The rain came down harder. "The cave will flood and we'll be stuck here." He moved, cried out in pain and stopped.

"I'll make a splint."

"You know how?"

"I'll figure it out." My voice was grim as the rain came down still harder and I looked around for saplings that I could use to immobilize his arm. The nearby thicket proved a good source and I soon had two sticks and laid them alongside his arm. Then I tore the sleeves from my shirt and wrapped them loosely around his arm. "Now can we go?"

"Of course." His puzzled expression said he didn't remember arguing with me earlier.

Silver came close and inspected Buck's arm. *"It's like my daughter's leg."*

"Yes. It's broken. We must get him to our own world so it can be fixed. So it will heal right."

There was a mental silence as she thought. Then she looked at me and, for the first time, I clearly saw the pain her daughter's injury had caused her. *"Can my daughter's leg be healed where you live?"*

I was pulling Buck towards the cave, unwilling to chance his falling again. He was now clear-headed but he was still sick. *"Yes."*

Her eyes said it all. *"Then please take her with you. Fix her leg."*

Just then the sky opened up, making the world as wet as if we were swimming in the pond. The cave would fill quickly. I looked upriver to where the creek bed disappeared up a hill. It wouldn't be long before it would fill, and the water would pour down the hill and into the cave, filling it. *"We may not be able to bring her back."*

She understood about the creek. She knew that when it filled the cave, travel between worlds would become impossible. *"She won't survive with a bad leg. Take her with you. Take care of her. Love her."*

"I will. I promise." I fought tears as I went to Tres. But she didn't want to come with me. She looked towards her mother when I grabbed her fur and tried to bring her with me. She whimpered. The other wolves, hearing, came close, protecting the pup.

Silver took care of everything. She moved among the wolves, nipping and pushing them away, letting them know this was okay. And she somehow communicated with Tres that she was to come with me so Tres stopped pulling. And all the while, Buck was waiting. I finally grabbed Tres by the fur on her back and Buck by his good arm. The three of us set off for the cave.

We stepped into the cave and the driving rain stopped pelting our bodies. I found Buck's flashlight and turned it on. Thankfully the batteries still worked. I flashed it ahead and we set off.

Tres came willingly at first but, as we retreated deeper into the cave and left her family behind, she changed her mind and no longer followed. She hung back and whimpered, looking for her mother or another member of the pack. Eventually, she sat down and refused to move.

I'd made a promise and, remembering Silver's heartfelt thoughts, I knew Tres wouldn't survive in Otherworld. I would bring her home with me and get her leg fixed. But first I had to get her there. I finally whipped off what was left of my shirt and made it into a sling. I then lifted Tres into the sling across my front and we set off once again.

In the sling, Tres was close to me and felt safe, so she snuggled against my bare skin and quietly accepted what was happening. Now all I had to do was get a wolf pup and an injured, sick man home safely.

It was easier finding out way back through the cave then it had been following Silver the first time we went through because this time we knew to follow the creek bed. Here and there, in the dry earth, we saw our own footprints still there from our original trip through. They told us we were going in the right direction. Even so, it seemed to take forever because, coming, we'd run through the cave. Now, going home, we seemed to crawl.

At first, the water came slowly. With the flashlight pointed ahead, I didn't know the creek was filling until cold water seeped through my shoes. I slowed, turning the flashlight behind me. What I saw sent a thrill of fear along my spine. Slowly, but growing faster as I watched, what had been a dry creek bed was turning wet. Soon, when the creek bed itself was saturated, the water would begin to appear and then, the creek level would rise. If we didn't reach our world before that happened, we might not make it. We might die in the cave.

"We've got to move faster."

Buck tried to comply, but the increased speed caused more pain. He grunted and tried to hide the hurt but I felt it in the way his good hand gripped mine harder. He began to tremble, whether from pain or the fever I couldn't guess. But I knew that if we didn't get out of there it wouldn't matter which it was.

I pulled Buck along. Soon we were running. That woke Tres and some of my fear got through to her and she began wiggling, straining against the homemade sling, trying to get out. If she succeeded, she'd run back to Otherworld and probably drown in the attempt. I stopped long enough to tighten the sling. She struggled harder but couldn't get free. I grabbed Buck's hand and, again pulling hard, I ran flat out.

"What's the hurry?" Buck's fever was once again taking over his mind. "My arm hurts. I need to rest." He stopped and felt the walls, looking for a place to sit.

Beneath our feet the creek bed became saturated and water began to appear ever so slowly, but soon I would feel it around my ankles. "We have to go, Buck."

"Don't want to go. Want to rest." His words slurred slightly.

"You can rest as soon as we get back to the boat." I pointed the flashlight towards home. I didn't want to give him any other direction to go.

"It's a nice boat."

"A very nice boat. The seats are cushioned. You'd like that, wouldn't you, Buck?"

He thought that over as the water rose to my ankles. I didn't know how much farther we had to go. I wished I'd paid better attention the first time through.

"Okay." He let me lead him, but he refused to run. He kept saying there was no hurry. I slowly but steadily increased pressure on his good arm, forcing him to move faster and still faster. Because, as we walked, the water rose until it was slightly above my ankles.

When it was knee high we reached the fork in the cave where I'd stopped and worried about which fork to take. It was where I'd realized we were following the river bed, where Buck had found a tuft of wolf fur caught on a rough piece of rock. "Not much farther, Buck. Let's hurry a little faster."

"We're going fast enough." I touched his body. His trembling had increased. I didn't know if he could make it. But he had no choice.

"Run, Buck." I had an inspiration. "They are after us. They'll catch us if we don't run faster."

"Who's after us? Who'll catch us?"

I thought fast. "The bears. The grizzlies will catch us."

Even in his fevered haze, he remembered our fight with the grizzly. He began breathing faster and sped up. Not enough to get us ahead of the rising creek, but it was faster than before.

I prayed.

The water was almost at our waists and Tres was feeling it and trying to scramble free of the sling as we reached the last leg of our journey. The cave entrance, the room that would soon fill with water. I struggled through the water, tugging Buck's hand and praying that Tres wouldn't get free.

I saw light ahead. Just as when we'd left our world in the dark and arrived in daylight, we'd left Otherworld at dusk and were now arriving during the day. If we could get through the last room. If we could reach that light.

The cave wall was higher than I remembered. When we'd followed Silver, we'd not even noticed the downward slope. Now, going the other way and carrying a large pup while helping an injured man, it seemed insurmountable.

We climbed halfway up before sliding back. Buck screamed in pain as his broken arm bumped into the cave wall. "I'm can't make it up there." He moved restlessly, trying to shake my hand off. I grabbed tighter and shoved Tres farther down into the sling. Instead of answering, I pulled Buck behind me and started the ascent again.

I heard water. From deep in the cave, the sound of rushing water reached my ears. "Buck!"

I screamed.

From somewhere deep in his mind, the terror in my voice must have penetrated. I flashed the light back where we'd been. It was easy to see the water rising in the bright light. "It's coming! The water is coming! We have to get out of the cave!" He heard and, on some level he understood.

He turned and stared at the opening at the top of the hill. He started walking. Instead of me pulling him, he walked under his own power and I followed. I struggled through water that was now almost up to my waist. I passed him and took his good arm and pulled him behind me even as I felt Tres struggle to push her muzzle through the sling in order to keep it enough above the water to be able to breathe. I prayed that she wouldn't push completely out of the sling and fall into the boiling cauldron of water.

We slid backwards twice during our ascent of that small hill but we didn't slide all the way back. We were able to catch ourselves because both times, I grabbed the rough cave walls and stopped our downward trajectory. Then I pulled and grabbed and scrabbled until we were once more near the opening that grew larger as we approached it.

An unexpected swirl of icy water hit us and suddenly we didn't have to climb any more or fight to get through the water. As the roar of approaching water filled our ears, we were pushed by the very water we'd feared. The creek filled the cave and sought a place to go, propelling us towards the opening. And outside.

We found ourselves in a rapidly filling pool just beyond the mouth of the cave. It was easy to let the pressure of the water push us to one side. Then all we had to do was climb out and sit on the bank and watch water fill the pool and spill over into what up until then had been a dry creek bed.

It would continue along the creek bed until it reached the tree where the boat was tied. Then it would slide down the side of the boulder and spread water over the tree that had managed to live only because of the largesse of the creek. Then it would continue falling into the lake.

We had to make the same journey. As we sat and recovered strength, Tres, no longer buffeted about, quieted down. When I peeked at her, her eyes were closed, and she slept. "We should get going."

"Can't we rest a bit?" Buck's face was gray, his shoulders slumped.

"We have to go now. Before we're too tired to do anything."

"I am really, really tired." I couldn't tell if his words were from fever or reality but it didn't matter, we had to get to the boat so I could radio for help.

I heaved myself upright and put a hand out to Buck. He ignored it, wincing at the thought of the pain of my hauling him up, and rose slowly to his feet on his own. "Okay." He indicated the woods before us. "Lead the way."

It was a slow journey but the only danger now was Buck's fever and broken arm and those things were helped as much by moving slowly as by hurrying towards help. Eventually, we reached the Delight. It was just as we'd left it, which seemed odd. So much had happened that I felt it should have changed, as if years instead of days had passed.

The marine radio worked. I called for an ambulance to meet us at the dock even before I cast off. Buck went to what passed for a cabin and found a soft place to sleep. His sleep was restless, though, the fever and pain from his arm still held him in thrall, but he was as comfortable as possible under the circumstances.

I found a rope and tied Tres to my seat so she wouldn't be tempted to jump overboard, but I needn't have worried. The moment the motor roared to life, she jumped into my lap and refused to leave. I steered with one hand while I hugged her to me with the other.

She was suspicious of this new experience but she lifted her eyes to me several times and there was no terror in them. After the babysitting we'd done in Otherworld, after the grizzly attack, she trusted me to keep her safe. I vowed that would be exactly what I'd do. With the cave filled with water, returning her to Otherworld in the near future was no longer an option. Maybe it would never happen.

Chapter Eight

Buck came up from the cabin, waked by the engine. He looked at Tres as if seeing her for the first time. She'd been stuffed into my shirt all the way through the cave and it had been dark. "Why did you bring her?"

"To get her leg fixed. Silver wanted it."

He thought that over, fighting exhaustion, until he understood. Then he said simply, "Change her name."

"Why?"

"Tres means 'three.' Someone will ask about the other two."

He was right. "What do you suggest?"

He shrugged, weariness dragging him down, closing his eyes, curving his shoulders inward. "I don't know. She's white." He shrugged again to let me know he was mentally leaving. "Snowball?"

So Tres became Snowball. In a crazy kind of way, it suited the pup curled in a ball in my lap.

The ambulance was waiting at the dock and soon husky paramedics swarmed over Buck. He was out of the boat and in the ambulance in short order, but they gave me time to say goodbye. I held Tres ... Snowball ... to keep her from running away or jumping in the lake.

Buck eyed her, fighting the sleep that was threatening to take over now that he was home and safe. "Snowball." He pointed so I'd know who he meant. "The wolf. Take her to the wolf center. Show them the leg. They'll know what to do." As the doors closed on him, he added, mumbling as he fought sleep, "Use my name. Tell them I sent you." Then he went silent. He was finally asleep.

We watched the ambulance disappear. Then my family came forward and crowded around me. "What happened?"

"Why didn't you call if he was hurt?"

"What's that about a wolf?"

Everyone stopped talking and stared at Tres. Snowball. I didn't speak for a long time. Until now I'd not thought about my family.

My story had better be good or they'd not let her in the house. In our family, wolves are predators, not cute, cuddly white fur balls. But they were waiting. I had to say something. "We found her on the island."

My mother came forward and took Snowball in her arms. Snowball nestled immediately against her windbreaker. "She's so cute." She held her up and examined her. "I don't know what he was saying. She's not a wolf. She's a dog."

Will took her from my mother. I watched nervously. Snowball only knew two humans. How would she react? She looked towards me. I smiled and stroked her back and she settled down somewhat.

Will's voice was rough with indignation. "She's a puppy. How could anyone leave her on that island?

She's not big enough to hunt for food even if there was prey on that island. Which there isn't." Anger poured from him. He loves animals. Except wolves.

Snowball reacted to his voice. She whimpered and tried to get free. My mother took her from Will. "Stop shouting, Will. You're scaring her, poor little thing."

Jake laughed. "Not so little. She's going to be one big dog." He hooked his thumbs in his pants. "Little sister, when this not-so-small dog starts breaking furniture, you get to replace it."

I gave an inward sigh of relief. Snowball had passed inspection. She would become part of the family. "Buck thinks she might be part wolf."

Jake snorted. "He's a wolf researcher. He sees wolves everywhere." He raked Snowball's coat. "No white wolves in this part of the country. None this large either. The guy must be blind as a bat."

Will added his own thoughts. "He went to the island to find wolves and he talked himself into thinking this pup is one." He laughed so hard he slapped his knees.

They couldn't know the truth but it bothered me that they disparaged Buck. I'd thought the same when I'd first met the professor, but that was before we'd followed Silver through the cave.

I held my tongue until I could speak quietly. "He wants me to take Snowball to the wolf center. Her leg was broken and healed improperly."

"Probably why she was left on that island. Some bastard got hold of a pup illegally that he thought was a wolf and then didn't dare take her to a vet to fix her leg so he just dumped her where she'd not be able to return.

"With her size and that white coat, she's very distinctive. If he'd have let her out of a car somewhere, people would've recognized her and returned her. So he found someplace where she wouldn't be found. Where she'd die."

My mother reached over and patted Snowball. "She's sweet. I can't wait to get her home. We have a rug I just know she'll love."

I was suddenly very tired. "First, the wolf center."

"No." My mother shook her head firmly. "First we take her home. Get her used to us. Tomorrow will be time enough to take her there. Besides, they might not do the surgery since she's not a wolf." She turned to my dad who'd been listening the whole time. "Don't you agree?"

My dad is a quiet person, he doesn't talk much, so when he does, we listen. "I'm willing to believe she's not a wolf but the surgery is expensive. Take her to the center as soon as possible. Let it be done there before anyone has time to consider her lineage." His eyes were hooded, and he examined Snowball thoughtfully.

Mom simply said, "In the meantime, Jane is exhausted."

"I am, Mom. I am."

My brothers stayed at the dock to help my dad with the Delight so Mom drove me home with Snowball on my lap, eyes wide open but so silent that I knew she must be frightened by all the new sounds and smells. And she must be missing her family like crazy.

We both slept in my bed. I was filthy but she wouldn't leave my side. Short of bringing Snowball into the shower with me there was no way to bathe, so I washed up as best I could and dabbed the worst of the mud from her coat. Then we fell across the bed and she curled against me. I pulled a blanket over us both. And we slept.

The next morning, right after breakfast, I took Snowball to the wolf center. A rather tall, thin woman about my age was behind the counter. A student intern, I guessed, from the way she tried to look important. I put Snowball on the floor, after making sure the collar and leash I'd purchased on the way were secure. The last thing I needed was a large, white wolf pup charging about the place. Then I explained about Snowball's leg and told her that Dr. Portman had sent us to the center. "He's in the hospital. Broken arm and he's pretty sick."

"I heard about Dr. Portman. Pneumonia, but the arm is set and will be fine." She looked me up and down uncertainly, as if wondering what part I played in Buck's life and his work with wolves.

I tugged on the leash and Snowball moved beside me towards her. She looked at the wolf pup and didn't know how to react to her any more than she had to me. Several expressions chased each other across her face before she spoke. "She's rather large for a wolf. Are you sure she's not a dog?" She pursed her lips. "Did you say that Dr. Portman sent her here? Dr. Buck Portman?"

"The same. We were on an island looking for wolves. We found her. Dr. Portman figures she got left behind." I pointed to Snowball's crooked leg. "He thinks she might have wolf blood in her."

Her expression softened, and she forgot to look important. She crouched on the floor at Snowball's level and, keeping her arms at her sides, spoke to her. "Hi there, little one. Can I see your leg?" Slowly, she reached out.

Snowball bared her teeth and crowded back against me. She would have knocked me over but I managed to grab the counter. "She's usually friendly." I guessed that the pup had recharged during the night and now had her usual defenses up as well as being once again filled with energy. Last night she'd been too tired and frightened to snarl at my family. Now she wouldn't let anyone get close without being fully vetted.

The intern wasn't angry. "I guess she's a wolf after all because that's how a true wolf reacts to a new human." She rose. "I'll get the vet. He'll decide where we go from here." She disappeared through a door through which antiseptic smells wafted and reappeared a few minutes later with an elderly man in a white lab coat. She introduced him as Dr. Manning.

The vet whistled when he saw Snowball? "Wolf? I doubt it. Too large. Though she does have wolf blood in her, that's clear." But he repeated the intern's actions, waiting patiently until Snowball decided he wasn't a threat. Then he slowly stretched out a hand to her leg. She shrank back against me once again, but there was no snarl, and she didn't threaten him when he touched her.

Eventually he was able to run a hand along her back. Then he asked me to lift her to his examination table. When I did so, he slowly, carefully examined her from her nose to the tip of her tail. With each passing minute, his eyebrows rose higher and still higher and he finally shook his head. "She's at least part wolf, no doubt about it. But I've never seen one so large. And she's ... different. It's not just her color. Her muzzle is shaped differently than that of any wolf I've ever examined. Her shoulders are broader. And her tail is closer to a malamute's than a wolf's."

I didn't want any more questions. "I don't know about that stuff. I just know what Dr. Portman said. We're here to find out if her leg can be fixed."

"Of course it can be fixed and it will be." He rubbed her head affectionately. "We'll have you running with the best of them soon, little girl." He turned to me. "She'll need shots first, and a thorough exam. And to be cleaned up but those things shouldn't take long. Then I fix the leg. The sooner we get this little girl running with the pack the better."

I led Snowball to a cage. It was roomy and clean and there was plenty of food and water. I locked the door and started away. It was the first time we'd been apart since Silver asked me to bring her to my world.

She cried. Whimpered. Jumped against the door of the cage and cried louder. I ran. I had to get out of there fast or everyone would see me cry. But it didn't matter whether they saw me cry or not. Because they knew.

As I drove home, using one hand to smear the tears that crossed my cheeks so I could see the road, I wondered if the know-it-all intern had ever cried over a wolf. Probably she had.

I was glad no one was home. Mom was at work at the library and Dad was in the fields. Probably checking for army worms, he does that a lot because they are so destructive and appear so suddenly. I supposed the boys were working on the Delight. They'd never trust me to keep her ship-shape so they'd be going over every inch of the boat they used for charters.

As soon as I reached the house, I opened the front door and walked straight through to the back yard where I climbed onto the tire swing I hadn't used for years and just sat and let the tears flow.

Snowball was a pup. She'd be unhappy for a while, but she'd survive. It wasn't as if I'd sent her into a dangerous situation. What I'd done had been for her own good. So why couldn't I stop crying?

I finally gave up trying to stop the tears and stomped into the kitchen where I grabbed a couple aspirin that I tossed down with a glass of ice cold water. Then I climbed the stairs to my room and tried to take a nap. After counting a million or so knots in the pine paneled walls, I finally succeeded in dropping into a fitful slumber.

But I didn't sleep for long because even in my dreams my mind kept going back to Snowball. It was as if, even in sleep, I could read her mind.

Her thoughts were those of any young child in a

scary place. She wanted her mother and the rest of the pack. She wanted to go home. She wanted me. Most of all, she wanted someone to love her and keep her safe. Then, as if the door that allowed her thoughts through had been slammed shut, all of my thoughts about Snowball ended. Just stopped.

My eyes opened wide and I sat straight up in bed as I realized what had been happening since leaving the wolf center, since leaving Otherworld, what was happening at that very moment as I lay there unable to sleep. I hadn't been dreaming about Snowball after all. I'd been hearing her thoughts just as I heard her mother's.

The truth hit me like a sledge hammer. I shared a psychic link with Snowball just as I did with Silver.

It was the only explanation that made sense. I glanced at the clock and, yes, about the right amount of time had passed between leaving Snowball at the wolf center and the time her operation should begin. The anesthetic must have taken effect while I lay in bed and tried to think of anything other than Snowball, an attempt that failed miserably. Now I knew why. Because our minds had been connected until the anesthetic took effect and shut hers down. When her conscious mind was put to sleep, the link between us was severed.

I couldn't hear her thoughts as clearly as Silver's because she was a pup and was still young enough to think emotionally instead of rationally. Silver was the alpha female of the wolf pack. Her mind was honed and sharp and her thoughts reflected that. Someday, perhaps, Snowball would reach Silver's level. But now she was a pup with a pup's thoughts and fears.

I wrapped my arms around my knees and put my head down, realizing for the first time how close I'd grown to Silver during the short time we'd known each other. We shared something special and we both knew it. As I rocked back and forth and listened to the sounds of summer beyond the window, I missed her so badly that I hurt with a pain that was a knife slicing through my heart.

Connecting with Snowball had brought home just how close Silver and I were. I was glad the pup was with me. In some small measure her presence eased the ache of Silver's absence until I could return to Otherworld.

If that ever happened. I stopped rocking back and forth and promised myself that it would. The day would come that I'd return Snowball to her rightful home and, when that happened, I'd see Silver again. In the meantime, I'd care for her daughter.

Sometime later, a fuzzy awareness told me that Snowball was waking up. I headed to the wolf center to visit her. The authoritative intern had been replaced by a laid-back man of indeterminate years who already knew who I was and why I was there. "Jane Peterson." He came close, examined me head to toe, and shook my hand. Hard. "I'm Todd. I can tell you that the pup's fine. That's what you're here for. The white wolf pup. She's waking up. You can see her soon. Want some coffee?"

He poured us each a cup and steered me to a

bench where we settled down to chat. I wasn't sure whether he was being a good host or was cornering me for some reason of his own. A few sentences into the conversation were enough to know the answer. My radar shot up. "Where did you say you found the wolf pup?"

I must mentally screen each answer so this nosy man couldn't learn anything I didn't want him to know. "On the island. Dr. Portman can tell you more than I can."

"You were there. You saw what he saw." He swirled coffee in his cup in a too-casual gesture. "How did Dr. Portman happen to be looking for wolves on that particular island?" He added a spoonful of sugar. "If you know the reason."

"I believe he heard rumors." I peered at the man before me from beneath lowered lashes. Yes, he was fishing for information. I'd do what I could to prevent any further expeditions. "Legends."

"Ah yes. The legends of huge wolves." I nodded and swirled my own coffee in imitation of him as if I had nothing better to do. "Dire wolves." As if I didn't know what he was up to. "I've heard the rumors many times." Coffee swirled, silence grew and neither of us said anything until, realizing that I wouldn't take the bait and talk about legends, he finished with, "I'm surprised Buck gave any credence to them."

I shrugged elaborately. "He decided to check them out. He hired my brothers to take him to the island. They got sick and couldn't take him as arranged. That's the only reason I went." As if I knew nothing and cared less.

"Bad flu going around. I hear he caught pneumonia."

"And broke his arm."

"A bad trip."

"We found the pup."

"It's not from around here."

"I wouldn't know about that. I only know that we found it on the island."

"He didn't say where it came from originally?"

"How could he know that? It didn't come with identification."

Wrong choice of words. He pounced on my mistake. "Which is why it's so odd. There is identification of a sort. There are differences between dogs and wolves. The pup is a wolf, no doubt about that. The differences are subtle but easy for an expert like myself to spot." He poured more coffee and returned to the bench, sitting a little closer to me this time, leaning into me. I dared not move. "But that wolf pup doesn't come from this area."

"Really?" I was elaborately not interested.

"Too big and there are other differences. The doc noticed it too. I'm not the only one. So we're wondering where it did come from."

"The island is all I know." I rose and tossed my paper cup into a wastebasket. I didn't return to the bench. Instead I strolled to the window and stared outside. The wolf center was in a wild spot but close enough to Johns Falls that howls could be heard in town if the wind was right.

Tourists loved the wild sound. Locals were divided, some liking the sound, some saying it reminded them of raids on livestock. Like our neighbor, Lyle, who chased a wolf from the corral that held the colts born that spring. He shot at it and missed and spent the rest of the summer promising to finish what he'd started. The wolf never returned, possibly because of his vigilance.

Staring out the center window I saw evergreens pointing to the sky and a few birches swaying in the hot summer wind. "Think this drought will ever end?"

He got the message. Talk of wolves was over. "I hope so. It's reaching the point where a single match could set this whole area ablaze."

"Or a single good rain could end it in minutes." A rain such as had happened in Otherworld.

"No rain on the horizon, but we can hope."

Then the vet entered the room. "You want to see the pup?"

Snowball was still groggy but she recognized me. She struggled towards me. I looked at the vet. "Can I hold her?"

"I don't see why not. The cast is well secured."

She looked like half of her body was in a cast. I knew the size was necessary to prevent her from tearing it loose. I sat on the floor and the vet put her in my lap. Even still half asleep, she cuddled against me. Now that I knew about our psychic connection, I sent my thoughts towards her. It was a tentative connection but she heard. Looked at me for a moment. And closed her eyes in restful sleep.

"You are what she needed." The vet considered the two of us on the floor. "How long did you say it's been since you found her?"

"A couple days. Maybe three."

He rubbed his chin. "You two forged a strong bond in a brief time."

"Yes we did." Todd was listening so I didn't dare say more.

"Now this little girl needs her sleep." He picked up Snowball and placed her in a cage. "She'll probably sleep most of the night."

"Can I come back in the morning?"

The vet hesitated. "It's not usual. Wolves should bond with their own kind, not with people. But I think that in your case the bond has already been established. And we don't know where her family is. So I guess it will be all right."

Todd didn't like that idea. "Are you sure? Won't a bond with this woman hinder returning the pup to the wild when it's ready?"

A shiver went through me. "Snowball can't be sent into the wilderness."

"Why not?" Todd's eyes gleamed. He'd been waiting for me to make a mistake and I'd not disappointed him.

I foundered. "Because ... because we don't know if she's ever been in the wild. Other than the island, of course, and there are no large predators there. For all we know she was someone's pet and when she broke her leg, rather than take her to a vet and have to admit to having a wild animal illegally the owner dumped her where no one would know. At least that's what Dr. Portman thought."

"That would explain why she's different from the wolves in this area." The vet was thoughtful. "She came from somewhere else."

I pressed my advantage. "She's only a pup. What if she doesn't know how to survive in the wilderness? What if no local pack will accept her? They probably won't. She'll die. We can't let that happen."

Todd didn't like the vet siding with me. "She's still a wolf. She needs to be free."

The vet looked between Todd and me. He was a peacemaker. "We don't have to decide her future right now. She has a long recovery ahead of her. When she can run like the wind will be plenty of time to make plans for the rest of her life." Todd didn't like the answer but it was obvious that the vet was in charge in this place. I hoped his influence extended to wherever Snowball would be sent after her leg healed.

"She can come home with me." The words popped out. "Like you said, we've bonded. We have a farm. She'll love it."

Todd's nostrils flared. "Not in a million years. Wolves are wild animals, not pets."

We both looked to the vet. He refused to referee. He checked the clock on the wall. "Just about time to close this place. If you two will excuse me, I have some things to attend to." And he disappeared into an office.

Todd grabbed a light jacket, and headed outside. "I'll be back in the next day or so to check up on the wolf pup." He disappeared, anger shooting from every part of his body.

I waited for my heart to stop pounding before leaving myself. I'd not given any thought as to what would happen to Snowball after her leg healed. I'd not considered the possibility of not having anything to say about her future. I couldn't tell them that Snowball's mother had placed her in my care.

Leaving the wolf center, I headed for the hospital to see how Buck was doing. No reason to pretend we were only casual acquaintances. Not after what we'd experienced.

He was sleeping. I pulled a chair close and watched the rise and fall of his chest. He had pneumonia, he needed all the sleep he could get. I wondered if he, too, was savoring the luxury of a real bed even if his was a hard, hospital one.

His eyes opened. During the moment before they focused and he saw me, I wished I hadn't come. What would I say? What would we talk about?

"Jane." He smiled and that made everything okay. "I'm glad you came."

"I should have come earlier."

He shook his head, barely moving, so he was still exhausted. How hard had the trip through the cave been on him? Especially the part wading through ice cold water? "I'd have been asleep." The smile turned into a grin.

Buck Portman had a nice grin, an easy, comfortable expression. "And I suspect you couldn't have visited earlier because you were at home, probably sleeping."

"I was." I didn't tell him how restless that sleep had been. No reason for him to know Snowball and I shared a psychic link. Maybe he'd never have to know. "I took Snowball to the wolf center."

"And?" His head moved on his pillow.

"The vet operated. Her leg will be fine." I told him I'd just come from the wolf center and that Snowball was asleep.

He lay back and let his eyes travel over me. His brows knit. "What aren't you telling me?"

So much for not mentioning stressful things. Besides, he'd asked so it wasn't as if I was dumping on him for no reason. I decided to lead up to the problem gently but, as soon as I opened my mouth, the words tumbled out. "Todd wants to return her to the wild."

Buck's nostrils flared. "As I recall, that's not an option. The gateway to her world is flooded."

"He seemed to think that I can't have a wolf for a pet."

"Oh Lord. I never thought of that."

We stared at each other. He was already looking tired. Guilt swept over me. "Don't worry about it, Buck. We'll think of something."

"Something. Yes." His voice was fuzzy.

"I'll go now."

"You can't, you know." He was falling asleep as I watched.

"Can't what?" My head snapped up.

"Keep Snowball. Because she is a wolf and people can't have wild wolves as pets."

"I'll have her." My voice was hard.

His eyes closed. Then opened again. "It's the law, Jane." Then he slept.

I left Buck's room quietly and nodded to the nurses as I passed their station but inside I was seething. How dare anyone tell me I couldn't keep Snowball! Most of all, how dare Buck agree!

All the way home I sent out mental radar to see if Snowball would respond but all I heard was the wind in the wilderness and the cry of a pair of eagles hunting over the river that snaked around our farm. I knew that if I followed it far enough, I'd reach the lake where Will and Jake should be about done checking over the Delight.

At home I paced from room to room. My mind was on fire. I considered and discarded plans for a dozen ways to spirit Snowball from the wolf center but every one of them ended up with her at my house and that would be the first place they'd look.

But letting some uncaring government take her from me wasn't an option. If the world didn't want me to have Snowball, I'd take her and run.

Chapter Nine

My family knew something was wrong. They tiptoed around me until Will shagged me on the back porch. I was staring into the gathering dusk and rocking back and forth because Snowball was terrified, and she hurt terribly. I could feel her pain but I couldn't do anything about it.

"What's going on?" He unwrapped my arms from around my waist and tugged until I sat beside him on the railing. "And don't try to pretend you're okay." His long form blocked the sky and turned the porch into a precursor of shadow.

I tried to look around him at the last vestiges of sunshine and happiness and couldn't. "I don't want to talk about it."

"Is it that guy? That professor?" His tone turned belligerent, the big brother watching over his baby sister. "Did something happen on the island that you don't want to talk about?"

He was so right and so completely wrong that I hooted with laughter. I wondered how I could laugh when inside I was crying. "I wish it was that simple."

"Then what?"

"The wolf center said I can't keep Snowball."

His hold on me relaxed and he stepped away until he no longer blocked the sky. "Is that all?"

"All? It's terrible! I have to have her. She needs me."

"There are lots of wolves at the center. She'll be happy there."

"No she won't. And I ... " I stopped before saying I'd made a promise because how could I tell Will about Silver? The answer was that I couldn't. I couldn't tell anyone except Buck. "She's so scared. And she's ... " I considered my words carefully. "She's used to me. Me. I don't think she'll ever get used to strange wolves."

"Because she's white? An albino?"

"Yes." I almost thanked my brother for giving me an excuse for wanting to keep Snowball. "Animals can be terrible to any one of them that's different. And Snowball is scared. So scared."

"She'll get over it." She wouldn't, but how could I tell him that? "Maybe you shouldn't go back. Let her get to know the other wolves. Let her forget about you. She will, you know, if you give her time."

"I can't." I refused to meet his eyes, pulled my arms back around my middle and stared at nothing. Realizing I wasn't to be swayed, Will gave a huge sigh and went inside. No one came to the porch for the rest of that night even though it was a favorite place to spend summer evenings.

If I tried, I could hear them talking in low voices.

"It's a wolf after all. The center would know, and they said it's a wolf. Not a dog." Jake doesn't know how to be quiet, his voice was clear.

"We can't have a wolf on the farm." My father hurt for me, I could hear it in his words and in his voice. But wolves and livestock don't mix.

"It's a puppy." Mom took my side. "It's cute and loveable."

"What happens when it's no longer little and cute?"

The silence that followed stretched so long that I wanted to scream but after that they took their conversation to the living room where I couldn't hear the words, just the rumble of their voices as they continued debating Snowball's fate.

I waited until the voices stopped and the lights were off before going inside and upstairs to my room.

As I stared at the moon through my bedroom window I decided that maybe it was time to leave home. The deal had been that I'd save a lot of money by living at home while attending college. But I wasn't sure I could be there any longer. I'd quit school if necessary. I'd steal Snowball. We'd go somewhere. Anywhere. I'd keep Silver's daughter safe as promised.

I curled into my pillow and stretched out my mind to see if Snowball was listening. She was, though the connection was tenuous, a mélange of juvenile emotion. Of fear. Of yearning. Of homesickness. Of needing something or someone familiar.

Me. I was that someone, that something familiar. I was her connection to home. And as our tenuous communication continued, I made a promise to Silver even though I knew she couldn't hear. That I would take care of her daughter. Bring her home. I didn't know whether that home would be my house or Otherworld, but I vowed that she wouldn't be thrown into a strange, frightening wolf pack.

The next morning I waited until the rest of the family was gone before coming downstairs so I was still home when Buck called.

"I'm being released. I need someone to drive me home. My arm is in a sling and everyone at work is busy. You free?"

"Sure."

"I'd like to drop by the wolf center if you have time."

"No problem."

A good night's sleep and a heavy dose of antibiotics had done Buck a world of good. He looked almost as healthy as before getting sick and the cast on his arm hardly hindered him at all. "Not a bad break, thank goodness." He leaned against the back of the passenger seat and smiled as if my elderly SUV was pure luxury.

When we reached the wolf center, Todd wasn't there, and the perky intern of the previous day was. The one who must have decided that I was one of them instead of an outsider who deserved to be treated like an inferior being. Possibly because I knew Dr. Buck Portman, a person she clearly worshipped.

She couldn't bring us to Snowball fast enough. "She is so sweet. And cute." She lifted Snowball from her cage. "There's something special about her, and it's not just her color. Don't you think so?" She held Snowball out to Buck.

I pushed between them and gathered her into my arms. "Yes she is sweet."

Buck coughed discreetly to hide his grin but his eyes met mine over Snowball's back and stayed focused as the intern disappeared in a huff because I hadn't let her give the pup to Buck. Then he stopped coughing and patted Snowball. "I'd never dare cross that lady. Mia is one tough cookie. But I think you're an awesome woman."

I held Snowball closer until she struggled against my crushing embrace as I examined the warm feeling his words had brought. "I can be as tough as necessary where my family is concerned." Then something in me fell apart, my insides caved, and tears started. The next thing I knew I was bawling.

Buck took Snowball and hustled all of us out of there, leading the way to a grassy spot beneath a clump of birches. The grass wasn't nearly as soft as that we'd slept on in Otherworld, but the tiny area was private and clean and green. He eased Snowball onto the grass and she wiggled until she was safely between us, then I sat while Buck went down on his knees. She pushed her head against Buck's leg and looked at me. Then Buck gently rubbed one of my eyes with a thumb and asked, "What's this about?"

Were all the men in my life destined to question me? First Will, now Buck. "They won't let me keep her." I buried my head in Snowball's fur and leaned against Buck's thigh and bawled some more. "I'm getting your jeans wet."

A hand patted my head much as it had patted

Snowball moments earlier. "Cry away. It'll make you feel better."

"But it won't change anything."

I heard him heave a sigh a few feet above my head. I looked up. He was looking down. Our eyes met. I wanted to drown in his look, to forget all about wolves and Snowball and rules about wild animals as pets. Instead I just stared at him as more tears welled until he said, "Don't worry about it. I'll think of something."

My tears slowed, the ones already shed ran down my cheeks as I blinked new ones away, brightened a bit and sniffed a couple times. In the short time I'd known him, Buck had always told the truth. I trusted him. "Can you arrange things so I can keep her? You work here at the center. Surely you can decide things like that."

He rubbed the back of his neck. "It's not like that. She's a wolf and the law is very clear. But I'll think of something." He hoped he would.

He didn't know if I could keep Snowball. I fought more tears. "I wish she wasn't a wolf." His back snapped straight. He looked at the sky, the birch tree and Snowball at my words and something gleamed in the back of his eyes. "What is it Buck, what are you thinking?"

He rubbed his neck again and the light in his eyes went out. "Nothing. I had a thought, that's all, but not a good one."

"Tell me! What are you thinking?" I grabbed his shirt and pulled until he started to topple over onto me and I had to stop because his arm was freshly set, I shouldn't break it again, though, as he looked away and said nothing, I wanted to because, no matter how I begged, he wouldn't tell me what his idea had been. Whatever it had been, it had to do with my keeping Snowball and I needed all the advice I could get, so darn him, anyway.

He did what he could to comfort me. He touched my head lightly and stroked my hair, letting his fingers trail down my neck and along my shoulders until, realizing how it could be interpreted, he cleared his throat noisily and pulled back.

Then he clumsily petted Snowball until I patted the grass beside me and he slid down to join us. We sat like that for the better part of an hour, not speaking, just playing with Snowball to the extent that we could without hurting her leg and with Buck's arm in a sling.

Then, as it was clear that the wolf center was closing for the day, we brought Snowball back inside and, after making sure she was comfortable, we left. As we exited the building, I sent reassuring thoughts her way. She received them and knew she'd be okay, but she didn't like the place, she was still afraid, and she was lonely. I listened to her thoughts but I refused to cry again in front of Buck.

As we pulled out of the center, he asked, "Can I treat you to dinner? Payment for driving me around today?"

I agreed, and we headed for town. But the farther we got from the center, the more strident Snowball's thoughts became until she was howling in terror in my mind.

Buck's phone rang. He answered, frowned at the message he received, and hung up. Then he looked at me sidewise. "Would you pull over?"

"What's wrong?"

"It's Snowball."

I managed to pull over without going in a ditch. "Is she okay?"

"Yes, but … " He rubbed the back of his neck.

"But?"

He rolled down his window. "Did you know you can hear the wolves howl from town?"

"I do. Everyone in Johns Falls knows that."

"Listen."

I opened my own window and heard a howling sound. From the center, of course. "So? Nothing unusual about that."

"They are howling because Snowball won't quiet down." I began to smile. "She's unhappy and is howling and barking so continuously that the other wolves picked up on it and are howling too." He rubbed his neck again. "The caretaker doesn't know what to do. She's a volunteer and her shift is done but she doesn't dare close the place for the night with all that noise and Snowball shows no sign of being quiet."

We listened for a full minute. The sound rose and fell on the air. "Why'd they call you?"

"They hoped I could make her shut up. They want me to come back and try." The look he gave me was pleading. "I know it's a lot to ask. You've been driving me around enough for one day. They'll understand if I can't come."

"Let's go." I swung the SUV around and headed back to the wolf center where the noise level was awful.

We went inside. Snowball saw me and stopped howling. Gave a few short yips and tried to climb the side of her cage to reach me. Mia, the formerly haughty intern ran to unlock the cage and brought her to me. "Here. You take her. Please." Her hands were gentle and she kept hold of Snowball a second or two longer than necessary. She truly loved Snowball. I forgave her for all her previous antagonism.

As soon as she was in my arms, Snowball snuggled against me and quieted down. Buck and the other center people watched. "Let her fall asleep," Todd said. "Then we'll put her in her cage."

"What happens when she wakes up?" Buck didn't like Todd any more than I did.

"She'll be okay."

Mia snorted derisively. "I doubt it."

The vet was leaning against the examining table. "I'm not willing to sedate the pup again. She needs good, natural sleep to heal properly."

"Then don't sedate her. Wait for her to go to sleep on her own. Someone can stick around until that happens."

The vet eyed Todd. "And who would that person be?"

Todd grabbed his jacket from the back of a chair. "Not me. You're the one who doesn't want to sedate her." He headed for the door. "I don't intend to spend the night babying an overgrown, albino wolf." We watched as he sauntered out of the building.

The vet turned to Buck. "What do you think? Will she settle down?"

They were ignoring me. I decided it was time to make myself known. "No she won't." While they'd discussed Snowball, she'd snuggled into me and I'd sent out my radar to see how she felt. "I can pretty well guarantee that she won't sleep tonight if she's left alone. She's terrified."

"And her pack isn't around to comfort her."

Buck nodded towards me. "But Jane is around."

They all went quiet and looked at me until the vet asked, "If Snowball goes home with you, Buck, will she be quiet?"

"I don't know."

"She'll be quiet." I wished they'd stop ignoring me but knew it wasn't likely.

"If Jane says she'll be quiet with me, then she will be." I mentally thanked Buck for treating me like a person instead of a nobody.

The vet wanted to leave. He wanted to go home but couldn't until this problem was resolved. "Buck should take her home with him. If she howls in his apartment, it'll be his problem."

"She'll be quiet," Buck promised.

"Bring her back in the morning. I need to check her out."

We all left. As the vet climbed into his truck, he gave Buck a slight nod and mouthed, "Good luck."

Mia offered to stay at Buck's apartment overnight

to help care for Snowball. Buck declined and, with a downturned mouth, she left too, peeling rubber as she crossed onto the gravel road that led to town.

"Thank you, Buck."

"I didn't see any other option."

"They could have let me take her home. They could have noticed me."

"It wasn't that. You're not an employee of the center. They couldn't send Snowball home with you. They could get into a mess legally if they did."

I rubbed Snowball's head. She was happy, looking everywhere and trying to tear off the huge collar that was between her face and the bandaged leg. If she could, she'd get rid of both the collar and the bandage. I sent her a thought, told her she had to leave it alone, but she ignored me and continued to worry the collar.

But she was quiet. "She knows you, Buck. It'll be okay."

"I hope so." But he didn't sound convinced.

I stayed until late in the evening, making sure he and Snowball both had dinner and a comfortable place to sleep, Buck in his bed, Snowball on an old blanket in the kitchen. When I tiptoed out of his apartment as the moon slipped over the town, she was sleeping peacefully, and Buck was preparing to do the same.

I didn't even reach my SUV before I heard the first howl. The second came on the heels of the first and was louder. The third was followed by lights coming on in two nearby apartments but I ignored them as I dashed back to Buck's place as fast as I could run.

Chapter Ten

He opened the door on the first knock and I dashed past him to where Snowball had been sleeping and was now sitting with her head thrown back in imitation of her parents, letting the whole world know how unhappy she was.

"Can you stay?" As I gathered her in my arms, Buck stood forlornly by the kitchen table. "Please?"

"I can call home and tell them the situation. They'll understand."

"I hope your brothers don't come charging to rescue their little sister."

"Will and Jake?" I snorted. "If they think anything is happening between us, they'd be more likely give you a medal than come to my rescue." I bent over Snowball and laughed into her fur. "They share a bedroom and have been wanting me gone for years. They argue constantly over who'll get my room when I move out."

Buck's look said he didn't quite believe me but he didn't flinch when I dug my cell phone from my pocket and dialed my home number.

By the time I flipped my phone shut he was pulling blankets and a pillow down from a high shelf in a closet. With one hand. I took them from him and, following his instructions, opened his couch into a bed. He tried to be the perfect host. "You can have the bedroom. I'll sleep here."

"No, Buck. You're still sick. You need rest more than me. You sleep in the bedroom and I promise not to wake you for any reason at all."

He agreed though he didn't want to. "Snowball will most likely insist on sleeping with you on the couch/bed. She has my permission." He sighed. "She was treated for fleas and worms and everything else the vet could think of at the center so I suppose it's okay."

I cringed and remembered sleeping in Otherworld where we were kept warm by the bodies of three huge, wild wolves. "Should we be treated for fleas?"

His eyes gleamed, he knew I was thinking of that night. "Only if we start to itch, but I suspect we're safe."

"I itch already."

"It's your imagination. Don't worry about it. Take care of Snowball and let me worry about everything else, including fleas."

"You said something like that earlier today. That you'd take care of things. That you had an idea. About Snowball."

"Forget that. I didn't have an idea. Not really." He refused to say more about our conversation beneath the birch trees.

Snowball and I slept curled around each other as much as her huge collar allowed. Every time she moved, it hit me in the face. But I managed to get a decent night's sleep and woke with the morning sun blasting a hole in a dream of wolves and endless wilderness. I opened my eyes.

Snowball was inches away. Her eyes were closed but her paws jerked momentarily as if she was dreaming. I sent a tentative mental probe her way, marveling at how quickly I'd gotten into the routine of psychic phenomena. Me, who'd never had a psychic experience in my life until Silver ran through our campsite. Nor did I know anyone who had. Yet it was easy and felt right to reach for another's mind. I just thought about her and it happened.

Except, as our minds touched, nothing happened except happy, fuzzy, baby dreams because she was asleep. I was glad she was beside me, I was fairly sure if she'd slept in the center she'd have had nightmares. Now I felt her emotion but no pictures. She was happy in her sleep. Was she dreaming of eagles in the sky of Otherworld? Of the pack or her brothers? Of Silver?

I touched her fur lightly and eased away from her so I could make breakfast with some of the groceries I'd bought the evening before after making sure both Buck and Snowball were fast asleep.

She woke up hours before Buck did. I took her for a walk, using the collar and leash I'd brought from home. Several people exclaimed over her.

"She's beautiful. What breed is she?"

"What happened to her leg? I hope she gets well soon."

"What a beautiful puppy. Malamute, right? Is she

a purebred? I'm wondering because she's going to be huge when she grows up. I've never seen a malamute so large."

I mumbled replies, choosing not to spread the word that I was taking a huge wolf for a walk. A wolf that, when grown, would be larger even than the dire wolves that had roamed the world alongside saber-toothed tigers. When we returned after Snowball relieved herself and accepted love and petting from everyone, Buck was in the kitchen and thinking ahead.

"What about tonight? What if she repeats last night's performance?"

"Let me take her home to the farm. No one has to know she's not with you."

He rubbed the back of his neck. "I'll know. If anyone from the center stops by to see how I'm doing, they'll notice that she's not here." He patted Snowball, who was getting used to being pampered and licked his hand. "She's not exactly tiny. I can't say she's under the bed."

We discussed various options and finally decided to wait and see what the day would bring. The apartment grew smaller and smaller as time passed because Snowball wasn't used to being confined without her brothers or the pack to keep her company. The anesthetic was completely worn off and she wanted to play.

"We can take her to the center. She can get to know the other wolves."

"No!" I was shocked to hear myself screaming but it was how I felt.

Buck took a deep breath. "Give them a chance, Jane. They might take to her."

I didn't want him to be right but I couldn't have Snowball myself so we brought her to the center and introduced her to the injured and elderly wolves in the fenced-in area behind the center. The meeting did not go well. The other wolves didn't like Snowball and she didn't like them. Teeth were bared, ears flattened.

"It's as if she's not a wolf." The vet watched with interest.

"Or not of this pack." Mia wanted to rush out and hug Snowball but she knew that the introduction of a new member to the pack was a touchy moment so she refrained.

"Give them time. It'll work out." Todd was the only member of the little group watching the introduction who thought it would end well.

By evening it was clear that it wouldn't end well. Instead of a lessening of tension among the wolves, there was an increase. Snowball wouldn't live through the night. Or the other wolves wouldn't. Even though she was a pup, she was almost as large as the smaller wolves in the enclosure and, with her broad chest and strong legs and paws, she was already their equal in strength. Buck closed his eyes and tried to think what to do.

"We have a guest bed at my house." The more I thought about it the more I knew that it could work. I was determined to bring Snowball home with me and if that meant I'd have to bring Buck home too, then that's what I'd do. Bringing them both home now would be a start. "It's in an alcove off the dining room. There are French doors that can be shut to make it into a room. You can sleep there."

Buck thought it might work. Todd didn't like the idea. The vet watched their verbal sparring with interest but refused to take sides. I wondered what he'd do if Todd won out and Snowball stayed overnight and repeated last night's loud performance. But Todd didn't win, Buck did, and we three piled back into my SUV and headed to the farm.

Buck leaned against the back of the passenger seat. "This is getting to be a problem."

"Only until I get custody of Snowball."

"That won't happen. It can't happen. Because she's a wolf."

"A very unusual wolf. That should count for something."

"Don't count on it." Something in his voice said his mind was racing but he didn't share his thoughts with me.

I called the family to prepare them. When we arrived, they tried to pretend that this was an everyday event but they couldn't fool me. Will cornered me. "Is there something going on between you and the Professor?"

"Of course not. Don't be silly."

My dad worried about the presence of a wolf pup on the farm. "It could affect the farm animals even though it is a pup and some people say it's not a wolf."

"I don't hear the cattle crying."

"That's a good sign, but it's not definitive."

Along with everything else, they wondered if I was changing before their eyes. My mom put it into words. "I don't recognize you anymore."

"I'm the same person who filled in for Will and Jake when they were too sick to take a college professor on a week's expedition to a deserted island."

"No you're not. You're someone new. Someone different." She tilted her head and stared at me as if the odd angle would enable her to see me better. "I don't know what the difference is. The professor, maybe. Or the pup. Or just time passing and I never noticed until now."

I lowered my head and said nothing and soon Snowball pushed herself between us and that was the end of the discussion. But I thought over our conversation as I waited for sleep to come because she was right, I was a different person. Buck? Snowball? Or another world that I couldn't tell anyone about? There were too many secrets.

Snowball made herself at home. There must have been something about the farm, possibly the pastures on one side of the farmstead, the forest on the other or the river that cradled it all in a lazy curve that made her feel at home. Most of all, she didn't chase the cattle and they didn't seem afraid of her. And she didn't keep us awake.

It was summer. On a farm, that means work. The very next day, Buck did what he could to help. His broken arm was a clean break and he could do more than I'd have thought possible, though at first he worked only in the house. By the time Mom got home from her job in town, he had dinner ready.

"Are you bored?" My brothers never cooked if they could help it.

"A little. Snowball and I kept busy while you and the rest of the family did whatever farmers do."

"Got in some hay. Fed the cattle. Fed the pigs."

"You have pigs?"

"Two. For our own meat."

"I've never been on a real farm before."

"This is a small farm. Most farms around here are small. We need Mom's paycheck, and the boys also earn extra money." Will had turned one of the sheds into a shop where he fixed our farm machinery and that of all the neighbors. Jake was in charge of fishing charters on the Delight though Will helped out. It worked. We were comfortable.

"And now you have a wolf."

"I hope I have a wolf permanently. Or until I can return her to Otherworld." Buck shushed me with a hand over my mouth. I understood. No one could know about the world beyond the cave, not even my own family. When his hand left my mouth, I whispered, "It'll be hard not to say anything." I was used to sharing everything with my family.

"When it gets hard, talk to me." His eyebrows drew together. "Unless you've changed your mind and don't care if that other world is kept secret."

"If I'm to talk to you when I'm feeling stressed, then you'll have me visiting so often you'll wish you'd never made the offer."

His mouth quirked. "Never happen. You're a

surprisingly enjoyable person. Besides, I might need someone to talk to, too, and you're the only person around who can listen without threatening to have me committed."

That evening, after supper, the family convened on the back porch as usual. But as the coolness of the night began to swirl around us, my parents and brothers excused themselves, saying they had things to do. Buck and I found ourselves alone with Snowball on the floor between us.

"Why did they leave so early?"

I groaned. "Because they think we are lovers or might perhaps become lovers."

He thought that over. "Better than knowing the truth."

"It'll work out eventually, and you can leave. Snowball is a pup. If I can't return her to Silver's pack, then she'll be a wonderful pet."

"Wolves don't make good pets."

"Look at her. She's like any puppy."

"That won't last. As she grows, she'll become more like a wild wolf. She could become dangerous."

"Not Snowball." I didn't tell him that Snowball and I had a psychic connection. That she'd understand if I asked her to be polite so he didn't have to worry about her behavior. Granted, she wasn't an adult, like Silver. We couldn't communicate as clearly as Silver and I had done but I was sure that, as she grew, that would change. We'd communicate easily and clearly. If she stayed on the farm, she'd become an absolute angel.

Our minds didn't sync perfectly, but it was easy to

tell that she didn't want to be left alone. Especially she didn't want to be at the wolf center. Every day, we took her there and every day, she made such a fuss that the other wolves ended up making so much noise and we were asked to remove her from the premises. I couldn't have been happier.

Todd insisted that she'd settle down in time. Mia loved her unconditionally and fussed over her endlessly. Buck reluctantly began to agree with me that she wouldn't adapt.

He wondered if perhaps Otherworld was so different that being accepted by wolves in our world was impossible. He worried about it. "What if she can't join a wolf pack here and can't return to the other world?" We couldn't agree on what might happen. And as everyone at the center discussed her future Dr. Manning, the vet, simply stood by and observed.

By the time Snowball's cast could be removed, Buck had learned a lot about farm life. "I'm glad I teach," was his simple comment when we were alone on the porch after the family had discreetly left us alone. They refused to believe our protestations that there was nothing between us and that the only reason Buck was there was because of Snowball.

We couldn't argue too strongly because doing so might switch the focus from us to Snowball. I didn't want to remind them that Snowball was a wolf and couldn't be on the farm unless someone from the wolf center was present. After all, earlier they'd thought she was a dog. So I figured that could come later, after I'd been miraculously cleared to have her as a pet and

Buck could leave the farm. Every night, I prayed for that miracle.

The miracle didn't happen. One day the vet took off the cast and Todd insisted that the time had come for her to take her rightful place in what passed for a wolf pack at the center. "We'll teach her what she needs to know and get her used to other wolves, then we'll find a wild pack for her to join."

"It won't work." Panic spread through my whole body. "She doesn't like them. She's afraid."

"That's why you have to leave her here and not visit."

"She'll upset them so much that they'll howl endlessly. You'll have to call me back to calm her down."

"I'll stay with her." Todd moved closer to Snowball and she bared her teeth so he moved away but he still refused to believe he couldn't be a part of her life. "Twenty-four seven if necessary. Until she learns where she belongs."

I looked wildly at Buck, Mia and the vet. Why weren't they helping? Why did Mia and the vet turn away and not meet my look? I concentrated on Buck. "You can't let this happen, Buck. You can't!"

Buck chewed his lower lip and fondled Snowball. She and I had a close connection but she liked Buck too. She accepted and trusted him. Now he had to help her. Had to! "Actually, I've been thinking about Snowball," he said in a hesitant voice. Everyone looked towards him. Buck was an expert and his voice was normally firm and confident. They all wanted to know what was going on.

The vet finally spoke. "What about her?"

"I'm not sure she's a wolf after all. Or maybe not a full-blooded one. Maybe only a tiny bit." He sounded apologetic. If I hadn't gotten to know him so well I'd not have known that he was acting. But I did know.

As I watched, I remembered the way he'd avoided telling me his idea, insisting that it had no merit, no value, and wouldn't work. Was he pulling it out now because he had no other options? Was that what he was doing?

He refused to look directly at anyone while he spoke quietly, still apologetically. "I was so intent on finding a wolf on that island that when we found Snowball I rushed to judgment."

Todd was angry. "She is a wolf. Look at her. Wolf ears. Wolf paws. Wolf stance."

Buck took a breath so covertly that I was the only one who knew he was girding for combat. I prayed for him to win. "But the size is all wrong. Color, too. And there are other things."

"She's an albino."

"Her eyes are blue."

Todd was disgusted with Buck's pitiful argument. "Not a complete albino. You know it happens. The blue eyes will turn yellow because wolf eyes do."

"She still could be a dog, or at least more dog than wolf."

"She's an anomaly but she's a wolf. She's an albino and I agree that she's different in other ways too. But she's a wolf, no doubt about it, and she belongs with others of her kind."

Buck's eyes flared. He was desperate. "So test her. Take a sample of her DNA and settle it once and for all." He turned to the vet. "A test should determine what she is."

I spoke. "In the meantime, she stays with me."

"I'll be there too," Buck added. "I'm certified to care for wolves." He folded his arms and dared anyone to argue further.

So it was settled. The vet took a DNA sample and Buck and I left with Snowball who wanted to run wild now that her leg was healed. I had to mentally rein her in and tell her that she should take it easy for a while because the leg needed to be strengthened.

She couldn't understand why she couldn't run free on a leg that no longer impeded her movements so we spent a long time communicating. It was so long that I worried that Buck would figure out that we had a mind link. But he said nothing, merely watched Snowball cavorting on the end of her leash, though he did flick an innocent glance in my direction every now and then.

Was his look too innocent? Did he suspect? I didn't know why I hesitated to tell him about our psychic connection except that it was too new, too fragile and I didn't want to say anything until I knew how strong it would be. I decided to divert his attention. "I'm so glad you're here, Buck. She can be a handful."

"We'd best get back to the farm to wait for the results. If your family isn't sick of having me around."

"They like you. Especially since your arm healed.

You clean a mean stall."

"I can't stay much longer. The school year starts soon."

"What will happen when the DNA proves she's a wolf?"

"I wish I knew." There was that something in his voice again, something that said he didn't want me to know what he was thinking. Hope flared, and then it died. Snowball was a wolf, the DNA would prove it and I'd lose her forever.

While we waited, I was insufferable. I had to tell the family what was going on but they didn't want to talk about it. As I told Buck, "They don't want to think about a wolf on the farm. They still want to think of her as a dog."

We'd wandered behind the barn where it backs up against the forest. There light and shadow chase each other across the weathered boards every time the breeze moves tree limbs even a little. We sat on the top fence rail with Snowball on the ground at our feet experimenting with her new ability to run. It was a good place. It was hidden from the house and the prying eyes of my family. If her wolf blood took over now that she could run freely, it would happen where no one else could see.

"You have to face reality, Jane. Snowball is a wolf."

"I know."

He turned my face towards him because I refused to face him. "You've won every round so far, Jane, but that doesn't mean you'll always win."

I started to pull away, and then stopped. His hands

framing my face were comforting and firm, as if they held the power to change any test results I didn't like. "Then why'd you have her DNA tested? Once the results come in, that'll be the end."

"Not necessarily." His hands dropped and he took mine in his. Then he looked at them, large and small, intertwined. Frowned. Looked away. "Remember, she's not of our world. So maybe he DNA is sufficiently different that no one will be able to say definitively what she is."

"We know the truth."

"We must keep insisting that she's a pet and was left to die and that I was wrong about her being a wolf because I wanted so much to find a wolf on the island."

"Will it work if the DNA is different? Will they believe?"

He dropped my hands. Loneliness swept across me like a shadow across the sun as soon as contact was broken. "I don't know." Snowball jumped against the fence, experimenting with her newly perfect leg. "I think it would depend a lot how different the DNA is and that I can't begin to guess."

I could sense her delight, feel her joy. She didn't know what the difference was in her leg but she knew she could run and jump better than before. Her happiness cut through my fugue of misery.

The vet must have pushed the DNA test through in record time. It seemed no time before we were called back to the wolf center. When we arrived, the vet was waiting, along with Todd and Mia. As we walked inside, I took Buck's hand and held tight. I didn't know what

I'd do if Snowball was taken from me.

The vet started off. "Snowball is a wolf. Maybe."

Buck brightened. "Maybe?"

"The results are puzzling."

We waited. Buck's grip on my hand tightened. Mia noticed and gave me a sympathetic look. Todd ignored me. "Puzzling how?" Buck asked in a voice so casual that speaking must have required huge self-control.

"She's a wolf but she's not a wolf."

"A dog, then, with maybe some wolf blood?" Buck was trying hard but his self-control was unraveling. I could hear it in the slowing of his speech, the pause for breath before each word.

"That's the most logical explanation."

"So we were right, she was someone's pet." The circulation in my hand was cut off as Buck unknowingly squeezed with all his strength. "Someone who abandoned her." I gave up trying to reclaim my hand and prayed that it would still be serviceable when he let go. "So I'm sorry we brought her to the wolf center. We shouldn't have because she's not a true wolf."

Still, the vet hesitated. "I think she's a wolf. My gut says she's a wolf. But the DNA says she might not be."

Todd was angry. "So she's a mutant. She's still and wolf and belongs with a pack."

Buck played his trump card, one I'd not have thought of and suspected he'd spent many sleepless nights over. "A lawyer would say that it would be your job to prove it and that could cost a lot of money." He took a deep breath and continued. "If it should end up in court and I suspect it will."

Todd's face sagged, the vet blinked, and Mia simply looked stunned. "Is this one pup worth the cost of a trial if the Peterson family sues?"

They didn't have to know that my family would never sue anyone over Snowball as Buck warmed up to his subject. "And when you answer that question, remember that the Petersons have lived here for generations and any jury would include their friends and neighbors."

The vet stared hard at Buck for a long time. It was impossible to tell whether he appreciated Buck's tactics or wished he'd disappear and take me with him. Whichever it was, he finally tipped his head towards Snowball and looked hard at me. "Take her. She's yours."

Todd disappeared into the back room, then outside, slamming the door so hard behind him that the walls shook. Mia knelt beside Snowball and gathered her in a hug. "Can I visit her?"

"Of course." I joined Mia and together we petted and pampered Snowball until she rolled onto her back and simply enjoyed being the center of attention. Buck and the vet watched silently, their eyes meeting occasionally then sliding away as if they didn't want to think about what had just happened. What they would have to do to become friends once more. What Snowball was or was not. Whether I now owned a wolf, a dog or something else entirely.

Then, when Snowball grew tired of too much attention and the two men needed a break from each other, Mia and I took Snowball outside and Buck followed. As we loaded her into the SUV, Mia said, "Will you be helping at the wolf center this coming year?"

It was a surprising question. "I hadn't thought."

"I know you're not a wildlife major but we always need volunteers. If you come around, I'll be able to find out how Snowball is doing."

"I'll give it some thought." I felt my way cautiously.

"Don't worry about Todd. I'll punch him out if he tries anything."

I looked a question at Buck, who said, "She's right, Jane. We can always use more help. And Dr. Manning would like it, I'm sure, for the same reason. If you come around he can keep tabs on Snowball. He still thinks she's a wolf, he just doesn't know what kind and he can't prove it."

"Can he take her back?"

"He won't. This is his center, he moved here to pursue research because of the large wolf population in the area. He knows how important the good will of the people in the area can be."

"Are you sure about that?"

"I'm sure." There was no hesitation in his voice, nothing he wasn't telling me. The battle had been fought and won.

Snowball was mine.

Chapter Eleven

It was one thing to convince people at the wolf center that Snowball wasn't a true wolf. They had to worry about lawsuits. My family was another matter entirely and, now that Snowball was mine forever, I kind of wished I hadn't used the word 'wolf' earlier in any context whatever.

"When you brought her here, you said she's a wolf."

"I didn't actually say 'wolf.' I said 'maybe.' It turs out that she's a tiny bit wolf and she was someone's pet."

"This is a working farm. We have animals."

"She's been here long enough for them to know her."

"Her leg was in a cast and she couldn't run. That's no longer true."

"She won't chase anything."

"You can't know that."

"I'm pretty sure. Besides, we've had dogs that chased the cattle."

"We got rid of a couple because they wouldn't stop."

"She won't chase any of the animals. I promise."

They left it at that but I knew that their side of the conversation continued when I wasn't around. I refrained from mentioning that I could talk to Snowball and tell her how important it was to be polite because they wouldn't believe me.

I could have told Buck but I found myself unaccountably reluctant to say anything. My link to Snowball's mind was too fragile, I was afraid it might snap at any time, and I didn't want him to know until I was sure it would remain and would grow stronger as she grew and we bonded even more than we already had.

With no need to stay any longer, he packed his things and moved back to his apartment. I watched, leaning against the doorway between the alcove and the dining room. "I hope you'll visit."

"Daily if you'll have me. Snowball is a wolf even if no one knows it except the two of us. I study wolves and she's a member of a pack from another world. Now that her cast is gone I'd love to observe how she interacts with the people and animals of our world." I knew he was afraid that those interactions could be of the worst possible kind and he thought that, as a wolf expert, he might be able to help.

For whatever reason, Buck spent the waning days of summer at the farm, mucking out stalls, helping with the haying and watching Snowball. My family thought he was courting me.

Every evening, we'd end up on the back porch where he'd input his observations into his laptop after my parents and brothers discreetly left us alone. We couldn't think of a way to tell them that we weren't lovers without telling them more than they needed to know. "Besides, if they saw what I was writing, they'd know that Snowball is a wolf who will grow larger than any other wolf alive today. Larger than the dire wolves of old." He slapped his laptop shut, the day's observations noted. "I doubt they'd want her here."

"By the time they figure it out, they'll be in love with her and will know that she's a perfect lady."

"I hope. If it happens that way. But remember that she needs exercise. She needs to run. And wolves are predators, it's in their genes. I'm not sure that you can counter her natural instincts."

"Not a problem." Because our mental connection was growing stronger all the time. As Snowball grew beyond the puppy stage, her mind sharpened and our thoughts linked easier. As we talked, she lay at our feet, curled in a ball, but that ball was noticeably larger than when I'd carried her through the cave in a home-made sling. If she'd been as large then as she was now, we'd not have made it. But, large or small, she was still the same, cuddly, loving animal.

I touched her with a toe. She lifted her head in response and our eyes met. Hers were still the blue of a young wolf. According to Buck, they'd probably stay blue forever because of her albino genes.

Her head lifted higher and she sniffed the wind that came around the corner of the house. It originated in the forest that butted the yard. Something in that forest had caught her attention. She rose.

"Snowball." My voice was stern. I didn't like the way she zeroed in on whatever scent was carried to her. She ignored me, slowly standing and moving closer to the corner of the porch the better to take in the interesting scent.

I sent out a mental order. *Stay! Don't chase after it!* She looked my way, her muzzle high and our glances locked. I felt the conflict in her mind and sent a third, stern warning. *Danger! Stay here!"* A puppy thought said she wanted to chase whatever it was. She wanted to find out where that interesting scent led. But some of my panic must have gotten through because, after a moment, she lay back down and put her head on my feet.

"What was that about?" Buck's lazy voice broke into my thoughts.

"She must have smelled something."

"Obviously." He didn't try to keep the sarcasm from his voice. "I saw that much. What I'm wondering is what got into you? I thought for a second there that you were going to explode." His voice was casual but his meaning wasn't.

"I was concerned. If she chases animals, my family will be angry."

"She stayed put. What I'm wondering is whether you had anything to do with it."

What to say? I wasn't sure our mind link was strong enough yet to withstand stress and I didn't want anyone to know about it. Not yet, not even Buck. "She sensed that I didn't want her to chase whatever it was."

"That's all? She sensed your wishes?"

"Like dogs do. They sense things."

"Dogs, yes. Wolves, no. That's one of the differences between them."

"She's not like other wolves."

He let the subject drop because night was approaching, and he wanted to get home. I wished he still stayed overnight as he'd done before Snowball was mine. It had been nice, our evenings on the porch had been filled with lazy talk about nothing and also the thousands of small things people discuss to pass the time.

I now knew that he was an only child and that his parents hoped he was happy. That he'd worked his way through college but gone to grad school on grants. That he liked living in the forest and hoped to stay permanently. That he'd be able to do that if he received a full professorship. That the decision about his future was up to Dr. Manning as much as to the college because Dr. Manning was important. That he'd jeopardized that future when he went out on a limb for Snowball, choosing her future over his own.

I told him what I thought. "When you risked your future to give a wolf what you thought was the best of all possible worlds, you proved you have a bright future as a wolf researcher. You proved you care more about them than about your career. And that concern should be a good indication of how your career will go."

He'd laughed without humor. "If anyone knew the truth, I'd be made to walk the plank. I'd lose my job and any credibility I've earned thus far. Fortunately, all they know is that I asked the wolf center to pay for surgery on an animal that can't be proven to be a true wolf. I'm not sure how the expense involved will affect my future."

"I never thought. I shouldn't have brought Snowball back. I didn't mean for your future to be ruined because of her."

"The decision was mine. I sent you to the center and told you what to say. I'll stand behind every word no matter what it does to my future."

I moved closer and touched him lightly on the shoulder. I meant it as a sympathetic gesture. He turned somewhat and leaned his head on my hand and we remained that way for a long time. Then he said, "Thanks," and I withdrew my hand and we continued as before.

But after that moment, there was a difference in our relationship. I couldn't say precisely what the difference was, except that one day when our glances happened to meet, we didn't break away as quickly as before. And another time after a hard day working in the fields, we accidentally bumped each other as we walked Snowball through the forest and we didn't jump away in embarrassment as we usually did. And still later, on another walk with Snowball, after pulling aside a low-hanging branch so we could duck under it, Buck took my hand and pulled me forward so I wouldn't be hurt as it snapped back in place behind us and he didn't let go until we were in sight of the house, a good half hour later.

As for Snowball, she grew. And grew. And grew. My family noticed. "Now we see why you insisted she's not a wolf. No wolf is that huge. There aren't many breeds of dogs that are that large. She must be a mixture of every huge dog on earth."

"We'll never know."

"Her leg healed perfectly. She can run like the wind." My mom loved Snowball unconditionally and my brothers enjoyed the bragging rights a huge, white dog accorded them when they were having a beer at Mickey's Bar and Eatery. Because of them, Snowball soon was something of a local celebrity. A topic of conversation. A legend.

"She's one of those wolves people talk about."

"She's not a wolf. She's a dog." My brothers were definite. "The wolf center had her tested."

"What kind of dog is that big?"

"Obviously there's some weird breed somewhere that's that big but no wolves, that's for sure." Will snorted in derision and the speaker shut up.

Opinions on Snowball were divided. Often while walking her in town, were stopped by people petting her and saying what a sweetheart she was and that they wished they had a dog like her. Others crossed the street to avoid us.

One day, on a walk through the woods near the farm a week before school was to begin, I told Buck I wanted to let her run free. "She's been on a leash long enough. She's a large animal and needs to run."

"Are you sure you can control her?"

"She always comes when I call."

"On the farm. This is the forest."

I unsnapped the leash, confident of Snowball's behavior, but I sent a thought her way to reinforce that belief. *"Be good."*

We were close to the road. The sound of a truck reminded me that my dad was returning from auction with a half dozen sheep. We watched as the truck pulled into the yard. Dad opened the gate to the new sheep pasture and backed the truck inside the pen. Then he made a shooing motion and the sheep came out.

Beside us, Snowball went into high alert. She stared at the sheep. A low growl came from her throat. Her muscles tensed. I panicked. *"Stop! Don't hurt them! They belong here!"*

She didn't hear. The connection between our minds had disappeared. Or she'd shut it off.

Her eyes narrowed as she prepared to go after the sheep. Buck, seeing what was happening, fell on her, taking her to the ground. And, just like that, the link between our minds returned and she heard me. And relaxed. The moment was over.

Buck snapped the leash back in place and said mildly, "I don't think she's ready to run free just yet."

I dropped to the ground and leaned against a tree, as limp as a wet noodle and glad my dad hadn't noticed us in the trees. "Snowball could have killed those sheep."

"It didn't happen."

"You were right. I can't let her run free."

"Not yet." He tried to keep the grimness from his

voice but I heard it and knew Snowball's life wasn't going to be as carefree as I'd thought. "Maybe with training."

"We'll work on it."

We sat on the forest floor with Snowball beside us for a long time. Eventually Buck gave me the leash and we got up and returned to the farm and he went back to his apartment.

I asked my dad why he'd gotten the sheep. "Neighbor was getting rid of them. The price was good and they are kind of cute. So I got them."

"Do you think it was a good idea?"

"Because of Snowball?" He stared at me. Hard. "Is that what you're asking?"

"No, of course not." But I'm a poor liar.

"Snowball is a dog. That's what you said."

"She has some wolf in her. A tiny bit."

"Half the dogs in this county have some wolf in them. That doesn't make them bad dogs and a touch of wolf in Snowball shouldn't make her any different than those other dogs." He watched my face carefully. "Should it?"

I said nothing more but I had a hard time sleeping that night because I kept going into Snowball's mind to try to figure out what had happened and what I could do to prevent it from happening again. But Snowball was a puppy and we didn't share as solid a link as Silver and I did. She'd forgotten the incident, it had meant nothing to her. I decided that I'd do what I could. I'd watch her carefully. But I was no longer sure I could keep her safe from herself.

Chapter Twelve

The weekend before school started, Buck became a full professor. "Due in large part to Snowball. Seems Dr. Manning liked the way I handled the situation, sticking up for what I believed was right and insisting on a DNA test even though it proved Snowball wasn't pure wolf and my theory about the wolf legend was proved wrong."

"Will you stay at Weatherby College?" He was the only other human being who knew about Otherworld and the wolves. Who knew Snowball's true origins. Who could help me with any problems that might arise. I didn't want him to leave.

"I'm looking at a house to buy as we speak. It's a half mile from the wolf center, smack in the middle of the forest."

"Are there wolves nearby?"

"Maybe. I know Snowball will love the place if she visits, which I hope she will."

He closed on the house at the end of September and the very next day, along with a few people from the wolf center, my brothers and I helped him move. Mia's eyes went wide when she saw my brothers, particularly Will. She stuck to him like glue all morning and finally took me aside and asked if he was in a relationship.

"Mia, I must warn you. Girls have been buzzing around Will since he was twelve years old. The thing is, he'd rather go fishing."

"So he's single?"

I'd long ago learned that when girls got near Will their good sense deserted them. "Good luck with him."

She followed him for hours, bringing him water and helping him move a chair until she dropped her end because it was too heavy. Will just finished carrying it inside without help and then went to get another piece of furniture. Eventually, Mia gave up on my brother and helped me scrub the kitchen cabinets so they'd be clean for Buck's things.

Todd didn't like any of my family but he worked hard moving furniture so I forgave him somewhat for being a generally unpleasant person. The entire day I felt pulled between the center people and my family. I didn't like the feeling because it made for an awkward day. I was glad when it ended, and everyone headed home. Buck tugged my sleeve as they started away. "Stay. Please."

"Snowball is home alone."

"Your brothers will take care of her."

So I stayed and we ordered pizza and that was how we learned that Buck's new house was too far in the country for them to deliver. I picked it up and Buck put a few things away while I was gone. When I got back he said, "It looked like a lot more stuff when it was in the apartment."

"You had one bedroom. This is a three bedroom house with a full basement and an attached garage. What did you expect?"

"I'll never furnish it on my salary."

"You're a full professor. You make more than you used to. In the meantime, close the doors to the extra rooms and forget about them."

"I could use one as an office. I can pick up a desk at Good Will."

"Now you're getting the idea."

We sat at his kitchen table and ate pizza and drank beer until it was way past our usual bedtimes. He eyed the clock I'd hung on the wall. "Good thing tomorrow isn't a weekday." I wished there was a reason to stay longer even though I knew I should get home. I thought he felt the same way. "I'll sleep till noon, but then I have a lecture to prepare."

"Wolf stuff?"

"Yep."

"Will you ever talk about Snowball in your lectures?"

"Nope. Never. Everyone knows she was in the wolf center until the DNA test was done. If I start talking about her in conjunction with wolves, people will figure things out and go to the island. Someone will find the cave and that'll be the end of the other world."

"I want to go back to Otherworld." He accompanied me to my SUV. I climbed into the driver's seat but didn't shut the door. "Someday."

"I know you do." I waited for him to say he, too,

wanted to return to Otherworld and the wolf pack but he said nothing. Instead, he swung the door shut but, before he let it close, he inserted himself between it and the SUV and leaned towards me. "Thanks for your help today."

Then slowly, inevitably, he leaned down and, after a hesitation to make sure it was okay, he let his lips touch mine. The tip of his tongue said he was thinking of more, but instead of proceeding, he backed away, shut the door, and waved me off.

After all, he was a college professor and, for a while yet, I was a student.

For the first time since carrying Snowball through the cave and into our world, my thoughts were so muddled that I didn't think about her as I went to bed. She knew it, too, curled beside me and watching through those intelligent, blue eyes.

Our psychic link wasn't one-sided. She could read me. Not clear thoughts, she couldn't read me as easily as I read her, but she could sense my emotions, especially after Buck's unexpected goodbye.

She was puzzled and perhaps frightened because for the first time, I was thinking about someone other than her. She whimpered until I brought myself back from thoughts of Buck and stroked her head. Then she quieted and slept.

The next day, she almost killed the sheep. Thankfully, no one saw it except me and the sheep were unharmed. But if I hadn't been there, they'd be dead.

I was taking Snowball for a walk without a leash

because we were on the farm and I decided it was time to trust her. The farm was now her world and the animals and people were her family. Only the sheep were newcomers and they'd been there long enough that I thought that they, too, were family. So when we wandered beside their pen, I ignored Snowball in favor of checking my phone for messages, looking for something from Buck that might mention last night's goodbye. I was at a loss as to how to react to what had happened, I needed a clue to what he wanted to happen next. But there was no text. No voicemail. Nothing.

I was frustrated and, as I looked towards the sheep, I didn't think to keep my frustration in check. Snowball's ears flicked up, her eyes focused on the sheep I was watching, her lips drew back over her teeth and she snarled. It took me a moment to figure out what was happening. In that moment, she attacked, moving at the speed of light towards the sheep who were too startled to do anything.

"Stop! Stop! Stop! Don't hurt them!" I didn't know if I yelled out loud or not. But my dad was on the back porch and didn't look our way, so my screams must have been mental. But my screaming didn't slow Snowball's headlong rush towards the sheep.

"Don't hurt them! Stop! Stop! Stop!" She cleared the fence in a bound and was in the sheep pen, rushing towards them as fast as possible with hundreds of generations of wolves telling her to attack and kill.

I screamed at her again, concentrating on sending my thoughts as hard as possible. *"You can't do this.*

Silver would want you to stop!"

The thought of her mother slowed her enough to give the sheep time to bunch up in a corner. My dad was still looking in the opposite direction with his morning cup of coffee, checking out the forest instead of the sheep, thank goodness. Another mental scream on my part brought Snowball to a stop. *"Silver wants you to leave them alone!*

She stopped, confused, staring at the sheep, cornering them, keeping them at bay but not touching them. But her ears were no longer flat, and her teeth were no longer bared.

At that second, my dad turned. Took in the animals. And came to where we stood. "Is she part sheep dog?"

I stood silent for a long time gathering my sanity so I could speak without my voice shaking. "Why do you think that?"

"She's has them in the corner but isn't hurting them. That's a sheep dog trait. Good dog you have there."

"Do you think so?" I managed not to betray my thoughts.

"Well, it would be a lot of work to train her and we don't need a dog for six sheep that are in a pen but what she's doing here does show potential."

"So we won't train her?"

"'Fraid not." He started to take another sip of coffee, found out it was empty, and went in the house for a refill. As the door slammed behind him, I let myself start shaking. I snapped a leash on Snowball and we went for a long walk in the forest where we could be alone.

On that walk I tried to get through to her that there were rules she had to follow and that the most important rule was that she had to obey me. She didn't want to hear about rules. Didn't want to listen to me. She just wanted to be a puppy and chase a flock of yellow butterflies that showered us in a shaft of light. So I let her and we rolled in the new fallen leaves and I hugged her hard, hoping my love would be enough if another crisis happened. Hoping she'd do as I asked because I loved her.

I didn't see Buck for a week, but when the weekend rolled around he stopped by the farm. "To see Snowball. You said I could visit." His eyes were asking a question. If we were still friends or if his goodbye kiss had been a mistake.

"I'm glad you came." We were still friends. He relaxed slowly and I'd not realized he was tense until then. Uncomfortable, yes, but not tense. Did he wish that he'd not kissed me? Or was the kiss irrelevant but he was glad to see me again? And did he come to see Snowball or me? "Snowball missed you."

He took a tentative step closer and I did nothing to stop him as he spoke in a clumsy way. "It's been a week. Even though school has started and everything is different, I still keep looking for you. Turning around and expecting to see you because I've gotten used to you being nearby. It started in Otherworld. There we were joined at the hip." His words came out without thinking. "And then it continued when I moved to the farm. And you and Snowball haven't visited me at my new place." I didn't know if his words were random or if he was trying to get what had happened between us out in the open. "Now that we're not together all the time it feels odd."

"I've missed you too."

He laughed and rubbed the back of his neck. "Did that sound as dumb as I think it did?"

"Maybe."

We stared at one another and didn't know what to do next. Finally, he said, "Want to take Snowball to my place? Get her used to it? In case you ever need a dog-sitter and your family isn't available?"

"They don't know she's pure wolf so there might be things they can't handle if I go somewhere. Is that what you're saying?"

"Yep. I'm available to wolf-sit any time."

"There's something else." I got Snowball's leash. "I want to talk about something."

"The other night? I apologize."

My head jerked up and I found myself facing him wide-eyed. "No! Don't apologize. It's not that." I didn't even try to pretend I was angry because I wasn't. "It's Snowball. Something happened."

His expression said he'd known all along that something was bound to happen. It also said that, since I wasn't angry, he was glad he'd kissed me. As our glances held longer and still longer, I saw a depth in him that I'd not been aware of before, a difference. When our glances broke apart I knew that, no matter what else was on his mind, no matter what he was talking about, no matter where he was, somewhere in the background, he was thinking about me. About us.

I almost purred.

We rode to his new house in total silence as I tried to sort out my feelings. I failed completely but I did a lot of thinking about the man beside me. Originally he'd been no more than a charter to help pay my tuition. He segued into a companion when we reached Otherworld. Later he was an advocate for Snowball. Now he was something else. I had no idea what that something else was.

At his house, he led the way to a brand-new swing in the back yard that he admitted to buying because he had no armor against an aggressive salesman who convinced him that he needed something new for his new house. It was wood and sturdy and designed for four people, two on each side facing each other.

Sitting in that swing as it moved back and forth while swigging a can of pop as Snowball played with a ball a few feet away, I told him about the sheep. I told him everything except the part about my commands to her being mental instead of verbal. I let him think I'd called to her out loud.

He wasn't as disturbed as I expected. "Don't read too much into it, Jane. The important thing is that when you told her to stop, she did."

"Not at first she didn't."

"That's normal for dogs, cats and every other animal including wolf pups. Especially wolf pups." He kicked the swing higher with a booted foot after making sure it wouldn't hit Snowball. He wiped a dribble of pop from a corner of his mouth with the back of one hand while I watched, fascinated until, realizing what I was doing, I looked away and made myself remember the sheep.

"I screamed at her. Loud." A mental scream as loud as I knew how that couldn't be ignored by either of us.

"Must not have been as loud as you thought or your father would have come running." My breath stopped. He watched and waited for me to speak but I remained silent. "You said he was on the porch. The sheep pen isn't that far away. I'm surprised he didn't hear."

I still said nothing. He put down his pop and turned towards me after checking to make sure Snowball was still nearby and not wandering away. "You didn't yell, did you? Not out loud anyway. Tell me the truth, Jane. You sent her a thought."

I shrank into myself. "Yes."

"Because you can talk to her with your mind, the same as with Silver."

"Yes, only not as well." My voice was scratchy, I had to clear my throat. He'd known all along. "She's a pup, maybe that's why it's not as strong a connection. Her mind is an emotional cauldron, a child's mind. She doesn't seem to have actual thoughts."

"But she understands 'no'."

"She didn't hear me."

"Or she was having fun and didn't want to stop so she tuned you out like all kids tune people out when they don't want to stop what they are doing."

"I don't know. I'm afraid. I need advice."

"I'm an expert on wolves, not on psychic phenomena." He rubbed the back of his neck. I recalled the gesture from Otherworld. He was unsure of himself. "When you were so passionate about keeping Snowball, I knew you weren't telling the whole story."

"She was so scared. She'd never been away from the pack." He touched my hair and breathed a sigh that didn't give me a clue about his thoughts. "She needed to be with someone she knew."

"She doesn't have clear thoughts and yet you got that from her mind?"

"I got her fear. I felt it. She was so terrified that I was afraid too. I couldn't go to sleep because of her fear."

"But you couldn't read her thoughts when she went after the sheep?"

"At first I could, sort of. Then her mind went blank. I got no thoughts from her at all once she focused on them, no emotions, nothing. But I did have other things on my mind so maybe that made a difference. I was distracted so maybe that made it harder for me to read her."

"Or she turned you off because she's a pup and didn't want to stop."

"I was frustrated so I wasn't paying attention as I should have."

"It's possible that she thought your frustration was caused by the sheep. They are animals she thinks of as prey. Animals that would be prey in Otherworld.

Perhaps she was trying to help you hunt. That's what wolves do. They are pack animals, they cooperate to find and bring down prey. Maybe she was doing what she thought you wanted her to do."

"Maybe." I slipped into a reverie to try to sort it out.

Buck's hand touched my hair again, bringing me back to the present. "I'm curious, Jane. If I'm right and she acted on your frustration, what was it that was so important to you that it sent her after the sheep?"

"I was checking my cell for messages."

"That doesn't sound so frustrating."

"I was hoping for a particular message and it wasn't there."

"School?"

"No."

The swing was so new that it didn't creak. Right then I wished it did so there would be some sound in the world. As it was, silence sat around us. Even Snowball was still, watching me, knowing I was feeling an emotion she didn't understand. Not a bad emotion, just a puzzling one. She rose and came towards me, whimpering. Buck stopped the swing and Snowball pressed her head against my leg.

"Me." Buck figured it out at last. "You were looking for a message from me."

I turned away so he wouldn't see that he was right but it didn't matter, he'd figured out what had really happened that morning beside the sheep pen. "I thought you might have something to say about your new house."

"Uh-uh." He shook his head decisively. "You weren't thinking about the house. You were thinking about me. More precisely you and me. Us. Because of that night. That kiss." He leaned around me until he could see my face. My eyes. My heated cheeks. "Yep, that's the reason. Me. You. Us. Hey, if I'd have known that was how you'd react, that all too simple kiss would have happened way sooner."

"Except you're a college professor and I'm a student."

"That's true. For now." He stilled the swing until nothing around us moved and even the wind died to total stillness. Then he waited for me to kiss him because he knew that if he waited long enough, I would. And he was right. I did. Twice.

That was all he needed. Enough of going slow. Enough of me taking the lead. He took over until, quite a while later, we decided we'd best take Snowball inside before we forgot she was there and let her wander into the woods where she might get lost and chase something.

"There's no swing inside." I liked his swing and was glad that salesman had talked him into it.

"There's a couch."

"I suppose that'll do.

"For now."

It was dark when he brought me home, his truck loud in the silence of the late summer night. I was afraid the whole family heard our arrival.

The next morning, I learned that they had. "Got home pretty late last night." Will thumped the top of my head.

"Why weren't you asleep if it was so late? What were you doing that you shouldn't?"

Jake walked in. "Yeah, Will. You got home just before Jane." I thanked Jake for diverting interest from me. "I was in town but Jane wasn't there, I'd have seen her."

They were used to Jake and his all-night social life but I was different. I was the quiet one. So they turned towards me. "Where were you?"

I considered several possible answers and settled on the truth. Johns Falls is a small town. I had no doubt half the town knew exactly where I'd been and for precisely how long. "I was at Buck's place."

"Ah hah!" Jake was happy to have everyone focus on me instead of him. "What were you doing there, little sister?"

"I had questions about Snowball."

They went quiet. "What did you want to know?" My dad asked what they all were wondering. "And why ask Buck? His specialty is wolves but Snowball is a dog, not a wolf." Then, in an even quieter voice, he added, "Isn't she?"

I licked my lips. "She's part wolf. You know that. You knew it when I got her." My dad's eyes narrowed, and I knew he was rethinking the day he'd thought Snowball was herding sheep. Going over everything he'd seen. Wondering if he'd missed something. I couldn't let him figure out the truth so I continued with, "Same as half the dogs in this area."

Jake stood up for me. "She's right about that.

Some have more than a little wolf blood."

"Not dogs that live on this farm." My dad's words were too quiet and completely devoid of inflection. "We have livestock here. Wolves and livestock don't mix."

Jake answered immediately. "Hey, Snowball's a sweetheart. No problem."

Will agreed. "She can't have more than the tiniest drop of wolf blood." He slid a hand along Snowball's back and she wiggled in pure love. "Look at her. She's huge and she's still a pup. She's going to be the biggest dog I've ever seen when she's full grown. That size doesn't come from any wolf ancestor, it's pure dog."

"You're right." My dad's voice was still expressionless but he took Snowball's front paws on his lap and he held her head in his two large hands and stared at her. Scratched her between the ears. "Good thing, too." He laughed a little too loudly. "Because as big as she is, if she was a wolf, she'd be more dangerous than the worst dog I can think of." He hugged her and she licked his cheeks.

The conversation shifted to talk of the farm and the hay that had to be cut and in the barn before it rained. If it rained. The drought hadn't abated.

I hugged Snowball hard and tried not to shake in fear as the rest of the family left for their various chores. Which was why I felt the growl low in her throat and saw the look she sent after my dad. With a sinking heart I knew what was happening. She sensed the fear my dad's words had instilled in me. She didn't know what had caused the fear but she knew who was responsible. And she didn't like it.

I called Buck and asked him what to do. He came immediately and soon Snowball was between us in his truck as we went to his place. When we exited the truck, he cut right to the chase. "Snowball should live with me."

"She's mine. I love her and she loves me."

"You can see her whenever you wish."

"She needs me. Not just when I can manage to visit but all the time. She needs me when she's afraid. She's a pup and she's away from her family so she's afraid a lot."

"That's precisely why she shouldn't live with you. Because when you are afraid or under stress she senses it and her wolf instincts kick in." He waited for that to sink in. "You can't be stress-free all the time and you can't hide your stress from her. She's too sensitive. And she's too young to sort out which of your emotions to ignore." I didn't cry, but it was hard. "Admit it, Jane, she shouldn't be at the farm any longer. It's dangerous for your dad's livestock and that means that it's very dangerous for Snowball."

He was there and I needed a shoulder and somehow he knew that. He pulled me to him until my face was buried in his shirt. Everything that had happened since Silver's invitation to visit Otherworld came together in one hard knot in my stomach. I cried.

When the tears ended, I found myself on that sturdy wooden swing beside Buck with Snowball on the seat across from us. She was watching, those lovely blue eyes filled with sorrow for me. But she wasn't angry and she wasn't attacking anyone.

Buck reached over and stroked her head. She accepted the attention and wanted more, seeking comfort from him and he gave it to her. He continued petting her until her eyes were calm.

I sighed. "Yes, she should stay with you." Buck knew about wolves. More importantly, he knew about the wolves of Otherworld so he knew about Snowball. And she trusted him. "You'd better take good care of her."

"I won't let anything bad happen to her."

I sighed again and sank deeper into his shirt. "Your shirt is wet."

"Tears don't count." Yes, they did, he was soaked, but I appreciated the thought.

"Thank you for being so nice."

"I'm not nice."

"You are nice to Snowball and to me." Which was almost beyond belief. He was sitting on the most astonishing wolf research in history and not using it to his advantage. "Why are you so nice to me and to Snowball? Why don't you tell the world about her and the rest of the pack? About Otherworld?"

"Don't you know?"

"You could become the most famous wolf researcher in the world."

"You asked me to leave them alone and I promised." His chest moved with each breath, slow and steady and reassuring. I wanted to stay there forever but I was done with tears.

I raised my head. "You're doing this just for me?" I

pulled away enough to look him in the eye and saw that I was right. "That's wonderful, you know." On impulse, I added, "Thank you."

He tipped his head slightly. "I love hearing that but I'm not a complete altruist. I got some pretty amazing stuff from Otherworld. I learned a lot there and I can apply that information to the wolves I study here. Knowing Snowball, watching her, having her with me on a daily basis, will help immeasurably. More so now that I know you can communicate with her mentally. That's incredible wealth in terms of research."

"But mostly you're doing it for me." I pulled farther away, enough that Snowball jumped from the opposite seat to insert herself between us, wiggling until she fit. I felt foolish asking how important I was to Buck but I wanted to know.

"Until lately I expected wolves to be enough. To fill my life." His gaze rested on my hair. "Dumb, huh?"

"Yep." A tendril of something I'd never expected to feel spiraled through me top to bottom, along with a hunger for something. For someone. For Buck. Until the two feelings merged, and I had to look away before Snowball read my emotion and interpreted it wrong and did something scary.

What she did was put her head on my lap and close her eyes in contentment. Then she moved it to Buck's lap. Then back to mine. Buck examined her closely. "I think she's reading your emotions right now." A small grin turned the corners of his mouth upwards.

"She's happy."

"Because you're happy." He scratched behind Snowball's ears and leaned down to whisper in her ear. "Does she like me, Snowball? Does Jane like me? Is that what's making her smile?" Snowball reached up and licked his cheek. "Yep, that's what's going on. Can't fool this mind-reading wolf."

I scowled at Snowball. "You've got to stop doing that." I turned away only to find Buck's arm around my shoulders, pulling me close. I touched his shirt. "Your shirt is still wet. Aren't you cold?"

"Stop trying to change the conversation."

"You could get sick. Again."

"I promise not to get pneumonia." We sat that way for a moment. "Though I maybe should change my shirt. Tears are kind of wet."

"About time."

"If you'll help me find something to wear."

"You're not a child, you can choose your own shirt."

"I want to make sure it's something you like." A few seconds later he choked on laughter as he added, "Do you always roll your eyes like that when a guy asks you to step into his bedroom?"

"Yep. And worse. Much worse."

"I look forward to it."

Snowball led us inside. She jumped on both of us and would have knocked us down if we hadn't pushed her away. Her tail wagged furiously and she tried to follow us into the bedroom but Buck barred the way with a booted leg. "Not now, Snowball. Play time is over." He indicated that I should enter his room. "She needs to learn to be alone. I'm going to close the door with us on the other side and see if she makes a fuss."

He checked his entire house to make sure Snowball couldn't get outside. Then we both hugged her and went into his bedroom where we looked for a dry shirt for him to change into. But somehow we got caught up in the simple act of picking a shirt and it was a while before we found one. It was even longer before we were ready to leave his room.

When we emerged, the wolf pup was curled on a rug in front of the fireplace that had been one of the things that had sold Buck on this particular house. She was picture perfect with her white fur contrasting with the multi-colored stones that made up one entire wall. She was fast asleep. "She let us go into that room without her. I wasn't sure she would."

"She read your emotions. She felt safe. She knew we wouldn't let anything happen to her even though we were out of sight. So she knows that this house is a safe place."

"I still want her to live with me but I know she's better off here."

"You can visit."

"If I come as often as I want, I'll drive you both nuts."

"You'd be surprised."

So I stood in front of that beautiful fireplace and fiddled with my tee shirt, my jeans, my hair. I gave Snowball a dozen hugs and looked around for something to do, anything that would let me delay leaving, but there was nothing. Finally I blurted out,

"For Snowball's sake, I hope we stay friends for a long time."

"We will, I promise. Friends forever."

"You, me and an oversized dire wolf from another world."

Eventually we climbed into the truck because Buck had to drive me home. Snowball jumped into the cab without being asked. She knew she belonged, she'd made other trips in the truck. Or perhaps she wanted to be with us wherever we were.

When we reached my house, she wanted to go in with me. I stopped her from jumping down while Buck grabbed her to hold her back. A wave of emotion as high as a wall hit as she realized that I was going inside and she couldn't come too. I almost lost it. Then I took control of my thoughts. I tried to let her know that being separated would be okay. *"Don't worry, Snowball, I'll see you soon."*

She must have got some of what I sent because she quieted down, but it was hard to watch her turn to Buck for comfort when I went inside. A wave of jealousy hit hard in the pit of my stomach. Jealousy of Buck.

But as Buck's truck started away, I made sure I was feeling only love for Buck because, if Snowball could sense it... and I knew she could... I wanted her to know that everything was okay. So I thought about loving him. I concentrated with all of my being until I realized that it was easy it was to think of him like that. As if it was the most natural thing in the world to think of love and Buck in the same thought.

I ran inside and slammed the door.

Snowball's mind was still melded to mine as I evaded questions from my family and, later, tried to sleep. I curled into a tight ball, then deliberately relaxed and let my mind reach out for the outside world where the cool and almost total dark of a north woods night was descending, and then I reached beyond that night all the way to Snowball.

She wasn't listening for me but I could feel her emotions. Awareness of her fell into my mind like gentle rain. She was content. She was loved. I was glad for her and felt guilty for still being jealous of Buck.

But I wondered. Did she see us as one unit the way children perceive their parents as a single entity? Was that why felt secure with either one of us? It was a good thought, it relaxed me, and enabled me to fall asleep.

Chapter Thirteen

The next morning, Will couldn't find Snowball when he came downstairs. "I have a bone for her." He opened the refrigerator and rummaged inside. "Where is she?"

"With Buck."

His lips pursed as he pulled out a bone. "For how long?"

"I don't know. Maybe forever."

He shut the refrigerator door a little too quickly and then stood still. "Why?"

"He's alone. She'll keep him company."

"And you have us, you're part of a family, is that it? You're not lonely so you can spare a dog you love and fought for like a tiger?" I nodded. "You're a poor liar, Jane. What's the real reason?"

"I told you. I decided she's better off with Buck. He has a house near the forest, she likes that." I turned away so he couldn't read my expression. I didn't want more questions, I wasn't sure what I'd say.

He moved towards me, crossing the kitchen like a big cat intent on its prey. "What did he say to make you give her up? More importantly, what did he do? Did he threaten you? Did he say he'd make sure you don't graduate? Something like that? Anything? Did he?"

"Nothing like that." My surprise at his heated words was genuine and he saw it in my face. "We talked, that's all, and I decided to let her live with him. No pressure of any kind. Honest."

"Dad. You know Dad is nervous about her."

I nodded miserably.

He slipped the bone into a sandwich bag and put it back in the refrigerator. "When you go to see her, take this." He had more on his mind than bones. He knew how important Snowball was to me and that I'd not give her up easily. "You'd tell me if something was wrong, wouldn't you?"

"Nothing's wrong."

"You'd tell me if the good professor is playing games with you. If he's using his position at the college to pressure you into giving him Snowball. Or … " His eyes widened as a thought occurred to him. "Maybe I've got it all wrong. Maybe he's not pressuring you. Maybe the two of you have something going on."

"Don't be silly." But I still didn't look at him and he correctly interpreted my action.

"Ah hah!" He hit the table with a fist. "You and Buck! Who'd have thought? You gave him Snowball because … because … because you have the hots for the professor and you wanted to give him the moon, only he didn't want the moon, he wanted Snowball."

Jake came in, fighting sleep, and grabbed a glass of milk that he downed in one gulp. "What's going on? What am I missing?"

"Our little sister and Buck Portman, that's what. It

seems that they are an item."

"Really? Where have you been, big brother?" He took another long swig of milk, ignoring the glass and drinking it straight from the jug. "That's not news." He let that statement swirl around. "Unless it means we're about to get a genuine college professor in the family. That would be news." He shuddered. "Guess we'll survive."

"It means nothing of the sort." I backed out of the kitchen. "This is a madhouse and I'm leaving."

Will grabbed the bag with the bone and tossed it at me. "Don't forget Snowball's bone."

"I didn't say where I'm going."

"Didn't have to, little sister. Now that you've given the good professor your dog, I know where you're going. To see her. Or him." He joined Jake. "What do you think, Jake? Will it be a spring wedding?" Jake looked from one of us to the other, unsure whom to side with. "Or would summer be better?"

Jake spilled his milk and Will doubled over laughing. I fled to my SUV and peeled out of the driveway. I headed straight to Buck's house because I missed Snowball and she missed me. I could feel her loneliness because the link between us was growing stronger and she was used to seeing me every day. Wanted to see me every day. Needed to. I told myself that I wasn't going for any other reason. Definitely not because of Buck.

As soon as I arrived I gave up pretending and admitted that I wanted to see Buck as much as I did Snowball and was glad when both tumbled out of the house at the same time to greet me. Snowball got to me first. I was hugging her when Buck reached us and stood back and waited to be acknowledged.

Snowball curled into a ball between us and refused to be ignored but Buck did a pretty good job of it, looking at me instead of at her. "This was a heartwarming welcome scene. Ready to move in yet?"

I laughed. "I didn't miss Snowball that much."

"Who said anything about Snowball?"

Snowball wanted to run. She trotted towards the forest. The only way we could keep track of her was to follow so we went after her and stepped into the cool, secret world beyond Buck's back yard. A world of predators and prey. Of wolves and deer. A world like the one Snowball had been born into and where she belonged.

Buck grabbed my hand and we raced after her as she failed to catch a butterfly, then did catch a frog that she ate in one gulp, much to my disgust. Next she inspected a dead log. "I hope there aren't any grub worms in it."

"Grub worms are protein."

"Ugh."

Her head went up. Her ears pricked. She turned one way and then another. Then she started running. It was all we could do to keep up or soon we would lose her. "What's she after?"

"I can't see."

She stopped and froze. A fair-sized doe was eating grass in a tiny clearing. Her ears flicked back and forth but the wind blew towards us so she couldn't get our scent and Snowball was no longer moving so the doe didn't see her.

"She mustn't chase deer."

Snowball let out a low growl and her muscles tensed. The doe, finally hearing the sound, was off in a single bound. Snowball paused long enough to look our way. We were family. We were part of the pack. "She thinks we're hunting. She's asking for instructions."

"We have to stop her."

"*You* have to stop her, Jane. You. With your mind." Buck squeezed my hand. He reached for me. He wanted to help but couldn't.

She hadn't listened to me when she went after the sheep. But I now knew what she was doing. I knew she was hunting with her pack. I sent my mind towards hers, grabbed Buck's hand back, and thought as hard as I could. *"Don't chase it! Don't kill it! We don't need meat."*

She wagged her head several times, trying to shake my thoughts away. She wanted to chase the deer and take it down. It was what the pack did, it was what she'd been learning when we took her from her family. It was her life, her heritage, her right.

She whined. She cried. She made circles from the clearing to us and back again. But she didn't chase the doe. Finally, it was far enough away that there was no chance of catching it. Its scent dissipated. She slowed her frantic movements, quieted, and stopped.

"She listened to you. She obeyed."

"She didn't want to. Next time she might ignore me."

"I don't think so. She's getting used to our ways. She's well fed, there's no need for her to hunt. So if you order her to stop, she will."

I was shaking. Buck and I were still holding hands, it was a simple matter for me to step into the circle of his warmth and lean against him. "Snowball's okay but you're one stressed-out woman." His voice was deeper than usual, with a hint of something that sent shivers up and down my body.

I'd push myself right inside of him if possible but he peeled me from his body, all the while keeping one eye on Snowball who had settled down and was once more inspecting the dead log. There was something in it that she liked beyond grub worms. I didn't want to know what it was.

I didn't like being separated from Buck even though I felt foolish for throwing myself at him. "I apologize."

"No apology necessary. But I'm thinking that Snowball has had enough of a walk for the moment and you need to sit somewhere long enough to stop shaking."

"I'm not shaking."

"Yes you are." He touched me lightly. I looked where he'd touched and, yes, I was trembling violently.

We'd reached his house when my cell rang. It was Jake. "Mom says to bring Snowball and Buck to dinner."

"Why?"

"Because we miss Snowball and, since she lives with Buck, he's invited too."

I groaned as I flipped the phone shut. Buck asked what was wrong. "My family." I passed on the invitation. "Brace yourself."

Dinner was in the yard because the weather was perfect and there was enough space that I could keep between Buck and every one of my family who was curious about him. Which was all of them, though they hid their curiosity behind pretending to play with Snowball. When the evening ended, my dad casually gave Buck a standing invitation to dinner every weekend. "So we can see Snowball."

"Glad to." When I walked Buck to his truck, he grinned from ear to ear. "Nice family you have." I sighed, slammed the truck door shut and was back in the house before he was out of the driveway.

My mom was clearing up. "You two are serious, aren't you?"

"No."

"Yes you are. It sticks out all over you. Both of you."

I went outside and climbed the fence and stared at the sheep until it got so dark I couldn't see them even though they were white. No moon, no stars and the air smelled damp. Was the drought ending? Would it rain?

Before midnight the first lightning strike came followed by thunder that shook the house and rain that fell as hard as the rain that had sent us running from Otherworld. That rain had filled the cave and sealed the entrance. I listened to the drops now pounding against the window and wondered if the cave between worlds would ever become useable again. And I opened my mind to Snowball's and knew she, too, was listening to the rain. And thinking of her home world. And missing Silver and the pack.

As I turned over and stuffed my head beneath a pillow to block the thunder, I was surprised to realize that I missed Buck as much as I missed Snowball though in a totally different way. I thought back to my mother's words and wondered if Buck missed me too. If she was right that our feelings showed in both of us.

The next thing I wondered was whether I could find out how he felt through my connection to Snowball. If our psychic bond would extend to something like that. I closed my eyes and tried to feel where the wolf pup was and where Buck was in relation to her. The answer made me smile because she was curled beside him. She was inches from him and pushing her nose closer each time the thunder boomed. She was on his bed and he was sound asleep.

The next day I decided to ask him if he enjoyed sleeping with a dire wolf. It was a school day and I'd spent most of it in a classroom and was in the lunchroom grabbing a sandwich before seeking him out. As I sat I thought about graduation and beyond. Would I be able to find a job in Johns Falls or would my expensive education would go to waste because I couldn't bear to be separated from Snowball by more than a dozen or so miles?

A shadow darkened my laptop and Mia dropped into the chair opposite mine. Soon she was rattling on about the wolf center. "We lost people, you know. Dr. Manning was a great draw. Students came from all over just to work under him. But now he's gone so fewer students volunteer. Those of us who are left will have to work overtime, Buck included." She sipped a cola and waited for me to figure out what she was talking about. "Buck is great but he doesn't have the name recognition Dr. Manning does. So we could use some help now that Dr. Manning is in Russia for a year." She looked at me expectantly as if I should know what she was talking about.

"Dr. Manning is gone?"

"Didn't you hear?" I shook my head. "I thought Dr. Portman might have told you." Did she, too, think Buck and I were an item? If so, was she right? No, we were definitely not a couple. Not yet, anyway. "Field work. Russian wolves are huge. Snowball might have Russian wolf in her and the good doctor can't get her off his mind. So he's off to Russia to search for her relatives. He took some of her DNA with him for comparison purposes. But he'll be back. In the meantime we're hurting for help."

"What kind of help?"

"The free kind. We can't pay so we need volunteers." I groaned, and she grinned. "I knew I could count on you."

"I didn't say I'd help out."

"That groan said it for you. Everyone groans when they realize they've been suckered into working for free. But we truly do need the help." She rose, her mission accomplished. "I'll schedule you for evenings and nights. All the day shifts are filled."

"How late exactly?"

"You might want to find someplace closer than your farm to stay on the nights you work, especially in the winter when the roads are bad." I groaned again. "Hey, Dr. Portman's place isn't far down the road. Just bat your eyes in his direction and say you want to visit Snowball and he won't dare send you away. If he does, you come to me and I'll tell him a thing or two." She left, finding another student to plunk herself beside. She didn't stay long, and her grin went weak so I figured I was the only sucker she hooked that day.

I showed up at the wolf center on my first appointed evening. Mia was there to show me the ropes. "First we clean the pens outside. Then the cages. Then anything else that needs cleaning, which is pretty much everything because we can't afford to pay for a cleaning service."

"What else?"

"That's it for now. I'm sure we'll find other things for you to do once we know your strong points." She found shovels for both of us and didn't pretend not to hear my softly indrawn breath. "Remember, you volunteered."

"I've mucked out lots of stalls."

She grinned widely. "So you know the ropes." But she worked alongside me until I got the hang of cleaning up after a bunch of wild animals and a few people.

After that I was pretty much alone when I worked. Often one or more of the wolf center personnel would still be around in the evenings, finishing up whatever they were doing. Buck, taking over for Dr. Manning as well as handling his own work load spent more time there than anyone else.

One evening, I found him at his desk with his eyes closed. "Are you okay?"

One eye opened. "Headache."

"I'm not surprised. You're doing the work of two people."

"It's not forever."

"That doesn't help much right now."

He wiggled his shoulders trying to get the knots out. "You're right about that." He blinked and bent over his computer to resume work.

"Want a massage? According to my dad, I make a great masseuse, the result of growing up on a farm. Cleaning a barn is hard on the shoulders."

"If you don't mind." He shoved the laptop away and closed his eyes.

His muscles were knotted. I unbuttoned his shirt and slid it down his arms, leaving only his tee shirt between my fingers and his shoulders. The last time I'd felt his back his bare skin had been feverish. Now he was comfortably warm and as I worked the muscles towards relaxation, I noted what good shape he was in. He must work out faithfully.

His eyes opened, and I realized I'd been massaging the same place forever, not thinking what I was doing. Feeling Buck's body, his skin, taking in the scent of him. I knew he used personal products without scent so as not to confuse the wolves. Everyone at the center did, including me. But there was something about his scent that I couldn't place, something that informed me that

I was near him. Was it that subtle something that normally only wild animals pick up on? Was it something I'd learned from Snowball? Was it how they differentiated one person from another? Or was it just me recognizing Buck?

I moved my fingers to another knot in his shoulders, dug my fingers in and kneaded until they finally relaxed. "Thanks." He didn't turn, just opened his laptop once more and took up where he'd left off. I went back to cleaning desks, working around the piles of papers that were growing higher with every passing week that Dr. Manning was gone.

When he left, the door didn't latch properly and swung open a bit later. I went to close it and stood in the doorway looking out over the changing landscape. Winter was coming soon. The yard that was now covered with leaves would soon be lost beneath feet of snow.

It happened. Not that night, nor the next, but in the coming weeks winter descended upon the north woods complete with snow and wind and cold weather. Sometimes, wherever the trees broke the wind, the roads were fine, and I had no problem getting home from the wolf center. Other times, when it blew from a different direction, driving was slow. Several times I wished I'd not volunteered at the center because the trip home in the dark was treacherous. But I never asked Buck if I could stay at his place.

Sometimes I'd babysit Snowball when Buck had evening classes. I brought her with me to the center.

She enjoyed such outings. Every time she came, she checked for new scents and investigated every corner and crevice. After a trip or two around the place, she always came to my desk to share her findings. Not thoughts, exactly, she still thought mostly in emotions, though as she grew her mind sharpened and became more focused. Our communication was closer to a kind of language though I realized that was unlikely to happen. I couldn't see her ever becoming another Silver but she was definitely growing into a mature, intelligent animal.

Todd noticed her growing maturity one cold winter night when we were both at the center. He was getting ready to leave while I was just starting. Buck was there, too, finishing paperwork. He'd brought Snowball with him. He looked like he could use another massage but I decided not to offer with Todd in the room. I'd feel awkward.

Todd stared at Snowball. "When I first saw her, I was sure she was a wolf." He'd cleaned out the pens and I was grateful not to have to do it. "She has wolf ears and a wolf's splayed legs and her chest is wide, like a wolf's chest." Buck was listening while pretending not to. "But now that she's not a young pup any more I can see the dog in her."

"Really? How so?" I knew Buck wanted to know what Todd had seen but he didn't want to ask because he was supposed to be the expert so his voice was casual.

"It's in her behavior." Buck relaxed and nodded to himself. He knew what Todd was about to say because he'd seen it too. But I didn't know. "If she was a wolf she'd have turned away from people by now. It happens, you know. Wolves don't have all those thousands of years of living with people that have turned them into companions. Snowball, however, is growing closer to people every day. She eats up our attention. A wolf would never do that, which means she's more dog than wolf." He came close. "I wanted her to be a wolf. I wanted her to be one of those huge dire wolfs of the legends. But the truth is obvious. She's a dog." His disappointment was clear. I hid my relief.

A sound caught my attention. Buck was across the room, pulling on his jacket and gathering papers to work on at home. Our gazes met, and it was all we could do not to give a shout of triumph that Todd, the hold-out, was no longer a threat to Snowball.

Buck zipped his jacket, threw up the hood and went outside. Snowball followed him into what looked like it might become a nasty storm. I sent a 'goodbye' towards her that she acknowledged briefly as she chased a few snowflakes, then she forgot me as she climbed into his truck. Todd left soon after.

Alone, I turned back to cleaning the center. It took longer than usual. Thoughts of Buck and Snowball slowed me down. I saw Snowball in all the pictures of wolves on the wall and I smelled Buck in the old, polished wood of his desk and wondered how it could have his scent when so many other people had also used it over the years. Until I stopped working completely and simply sat in his chair and let my imagination run wild.

It was approaching eleven when I finished. The storm had been building since early afternoon and had grown into a full blizzard shortly after Todd and Buck left. Now, as I looked through the window and across the yard, I knew I should have followed them out the door and gone straight home instead of sticking around as long as I did.

The normally brightly lit parking area was barely visible through curtains of snow driven by a wind that sent it sidewise with the speed of a freight train. Why hadn't I noticed? But I knew the answer. I'd been thinking of Snowball. And Buck.

There was no way I could make it home. And I didn't want to take Mia's suggestion even if I could reach Buck's house and I doubted I could. So I called my family and told them I'd be spending the night at the center, then I poked around looking for something to use as a blanket. They kept blankets around to keep sick wolves warm. My jacket would serve as a pillow. Nothing would be as soft as the grass bed Buck and I had shared in Otherworld.

My cell rang. It was Buck. "I'll be there in a few minutes." I said he shouldn't bother. "Don't be silly. The storm is just beginning. If you spend the night at the center you'll also spend tomorrow and maybe tomorrow night there."

"The roads are bad. Don't come. You'll get stuck."

"My truck will make it if I come now. Later, that won't be true. So I'm coming while I still can."

Nothing would change his mind. I hadn't eaten

since lunch and the prospect of a hot meal instead of crackers and cheese from a vending machine was enticing, not to mention that a real bed was preferable to blankets that smelled like wolves so I didn't try too hard to discourage him. I did what I could to make sure the trip wouldn't take any longer than necessary. I shut off all the lights except one and pulled on my coat to be ready when he arrived. I'd turn off the last light and lock the door on my way out.

That didn't happen. The power went off before Buck got there. I was afraid he'd not find the center without the yard light as a guide but in a short time the roar of his truck overrode the roar of the storm and he stomped into the dark room. He was all business. "We have to get the emergency generator going or the water pipes will freeze." He threw back the hood of his jacket and tossed his mittens onto a nearby table. "It'll only take a few minutes."

"If there's a generator here, shouldn't we stay where we'll have power?"

"I have a fireplace and a pile of dry firewood. It'll keep my house place warm and keep the pipes from freezing but only if I'm there to keep the fire going. Besides, Snowball is there alone."

"The storm is getting worse. Will we make it?"

"There's only one open space that we have to get through. A drift is forming but if we get done here fast enough and get out of here, we'll be okay."

In minutes the generator was purring and filled with enough fuel to last several days. We pulled on our outer wear and trudged through the blizzard to his truck.

We rode to his house silently with Buck concentrating on driving, fighting the wind in the open space and finding the road in forested areas where the main effect of the blizzard was layers of fast accumulating snow. The road lay somewhere beneath all that snow but the only way to find it was to aim the truck at the center between the trees on either side and hope that was where the road was. If he misjudged, we'd be in a ditch and would face a long, cold walk to safety.

Chapter Fourteen

We made it and Snowball was waiting at the door. She hadn't liked being alone and let us know it. "Hey, girl. We're here now." She butted her head against Buck's legs. Again I felt that tiny shock that she was becoming attached to someone else. To Buck instead of me. I told myself that it was a good thing because if she ever returned to Otherworld, we'd be separated, and this would help her get accustomed to life without me. Still I couldn't help sending out my mental radar to see what she was feeling.

It was a familiar warmth. I knew that feeling. I'd felt it myself. I tried to place it and finally, slowly, I realized what was happening. Earlier I'd learned about Buck by accessing Snowball's feelings. Now the process was working in reverse. I was seeing my own thoughts in her mind.

Snowball's feelings reflected my own because she loved him.

I'd flirted with the idea of loving Buck, thinking I might or might not love him, but all the while I knew that I wasn't ready for a serious relationship. Not even close. But now I realized that love and Buck were all rolled up in one neat package in Snowball's mind and that was only possible because her thoughts were reflecting my feelings back to me.

Did she get it right? Did she feel my own emotion correctly? I stared at dust motes in the air and wondered.

"Hey." I snapped out of my reverie to find Buck's hand waving in front of my face. "Is anyone in there? You were weird. I thought for a second that you'd stepped into another world."

"Nah." I went around him and dropped my jacket on a chair, using the action to avoid looking at him. Just in case what I was thinking showed. "I only know one other world and when I go back it'll be in the flesh."

"I'll go with you." He picked my coat up from the chair and hung it on a peg beside the back door. A neat freak. Could I possibly be in love with a neat freak?

"Sorry. Next time I'll remember."

"No problem." He turned and as he did, I bumped into his fullback body and started to fall. He grabbed me before I went down. I grabbed him to break my fall. He hauled me back upright. And we stood there with Snowball circling us. Around and around as my own thoughts bounced back from her mind. My own feelings. My heightened awareness of the room, the blizzard, the furniture, the fireplace that crackled as it heated the place, but most of all my thoughts of Buck.

"Snowball seems happy here." I heard myself saying inanely.

"Must you always talk about Snowball? She's well and happy. Can't you forget about her just for once?"

"I guess so." I thought that over. "Yes I can." It would be harder than he knew. It would mean blanking Snowball out of my mind but I could do it. I'd done it before and I wanted to do it now. "But first I have to know she's okay."

"Fair enough." His eyes darkened until they were the blue of a rain cloud. His breath quickened imperceptibly. I noticed because I was suddenly hyper aware of everything about him. How he blinked, how his jaw tightened, how he rolled his shoulders to ease a sudden tension in them. How he was impatient for me to get past my fixation on Snowball.

I slipped into her mind. She was happy, content. I mentally stroked her and petted her and cuddled her until not a shred of anything negative remained in her being. And I told her that I would be mentally leaving for a while but she'd be fine. All she had to do was be a nice dog and curl in front of the fireplace. I suggested that she might feel like a nap.

I opened my eyes to find myself staring into Buck's blue ones while, with my peripheral vision I watched Snowball trot to the rug before the fireplace, lay down and curl into a ball. She hadn't liked the idea of not being the center of attention, but she was obedient, and she was sleepy.

Buck noticed. "You did that, didn't you?" His eyes were almost black. They were deep, light-scattering orbs. I told myself that I should step back if I wasn't sure how I felt about Buck. I should never encourage something I wasn't sure about.

I stayed where I was. Close enough to see his

nostrils flare, his irises dilate, his pulse speed up. My own pulse synchronized with his, my breathing deepened even though I felt as if I couldn't get enough air.

He rubbed the back of his neck. The gesture eased the growing tension and I wanted to laugh because after our time in Otherworld I knew what it meant.

My breathing increased, I couldn't control it no matter how I tried. I felt warm enough to run out into the blizzard without a coat. I wanted the heat to go away and I wanted it to continue forever. I folded my arms and considered him. "You're uncomfortable, Buck."

"Yes I am." He scowled. "It's your fault, you know. You drive me nuts."

So maybe it really was love. Surely nothing else could make me want to choke him and hug him at the same time. "I drive you nuts?"

"You do, and it has nothing to do with wolves or psychic phenomena or alternate worlds." He was gruff, husky. He cleared his throat twice before he finished. "It's just you. Jane Petersen."

I thought over what he'd said, feeling better and better as the seconds passed. "Should I be insulted?"

"Of course not." He moved closer.

Scant inches separated us. I held my ground, breathing in that essence I'd noticed before. Not a scent, not anything I could recognize, just something that differentiated Buck from every other man on earth. From every other being that had ever existed. Probably because Snowball sensed it and reflected that sense back to me. Not that it mattered. Buck was who he was.

If he took another step, if he came much closer, we'd be so close an onlooker wouldn't be able to distinguish one of us from the other.

He took that step and then only millimeters of air separated us, so little that it was heated by the warmth of our bodies.

He was taller than me, I looked up when he spoke. "I've been thinking. In fact I've been doing a lot of thinking lately."

"About what?"

"Us. We're likely to be snowed in tomorrow and might not get out until the day after that."

"And I'm grateful to you for bringing me here."

"I'm glad I did." He rubbed the back of his neck again. "But here's the thing." I looked up. "I hope we don't end up hating each other."

"Do you think we could do that?"

Neither of us moved for a long while. Then we both moved at the same time. Not far, just far enough to push those few molecules of air aside, but after that slight move, there was no space at all between us. "No, I don't think that's possible."

I savored the feel of him. Closed my eyes the better to know him but at the same time I wished I could see him and drink him up. Wished we'd not wasted so much time talking about wolves. Knew that without the wolves, we'd never have reached this place in our relationship.

But he still hesitated. He wasn't sure about me. I

gathered my courage and said, "I followed a dire wolf into another world and I did so on impulse. I went because my gut said it was the right thing to do. Afterwards, I brought another wolf back with me, also on impulse. My gut was right both of those times and I trust my feelings now."

I was watching his face so I saw comprehension dawn and spread to the rest of him in the micro second before he wrapped his arms around me. Then I couldn't see anything more of him, nothing at all, but it didn't matter because I could feel him and that was a thousand times better. Though I shortly had to fight my way out of his embrace in order to breathe.

I caught a glimpse of the fireplace that was all that was keeping the house warm. Enough large oak logs were piled in it to burn through the night. Snowball slept soundly on the rug in front of the fireplace and looked completely at home.

Buck found some sticks and stuck hot dogs on them and that was how we cooked supper. Then we made s'mores for dessert. Then we dragged the mattress from Buck's bed to the living room and dropped it in front of the fireplace. And we spent the night not sleeping because every time one of us moved, the other stopped breathing. But somehow we made it through the night.

In the morning I lay beneath a pile of warm blankets that I didn't need because Buck's body was enough warmth all by itself. I kind of regretted that eventually a plow would open the roads and we could leave. I considered the driving snow beyond the window and wondered how bad the blizzard would be and how long it would last.

"Not long enough."

I turned to see that Buck was awake. "How'd you know what I was thinking?"

"Because it's what I was thinking."

He threw the blankets aside. Without his body for heat I missed them. With them on the floor on his side of the bed, I'd have to get up, too, or start shivering.

Soon we were cooking breakfast on the stove that, thankfully, was gas so it worked when the power went out. When we were done, and Snowball had been fed also, Buck took me on a tour of his home. I was curious to see what he'd done with it. I saw one furnished bedroom, one with a lone desk and one that was empty. "Someday I'll have this place furnished." The wind howled around the corners. "After this blizzard ends, I'll move the stack of firewood to the spare bedroom where I can get at it without going outside."

"Where is it?"

"Just beyond the porch." That was buried in snow.

"We can take turns."

"It's my place. My job."

"I grew up here, remember? I know all about carrying wood. I can split it too."

"You can use an axe?" He was awed.

"Of course not. We have a log splitter. It works great, splits a winter's worth of wood in a day."

Snowball was awake and wanted to play. At first she chased her ball eagerly, but as the morning passed she seemed to lose interest. "That's never happened before, at least not while she was at the farm. Doesn't she like her ball anymore?'

"She loves it." Buck had been watching her. "It's something else. She senses something." He went to a window and pulled the curtain aside.

"The wind?"

He shook his head. "I don't think so, it's been blowing all day and night without bothering her. It's something else."

Then we heard it. A howling sound. My stomach clenched. "Wolves."

Snowball went to the window. She'd grown so large that all she had to do was put her paws on the sill to easily see outside. Not that there was anything to see except endless snow still ghosting sidewise across the window. But she knew there was something out there. Her body tensed as she listened with every fiber of her being.

The howls came again, this time closer than before. Louder. More frightening. "More than one wolf." Buck knew wolves. "A pack."

"Are they here for Snowball?"

"More likely they are hunting. The blizzard provides perfect cover and deer have a hard time moving through the snow. Wolves have large paws, they can run on the surface. Deer sink in and can be caught easily."

"They are killing deer."

"And Snowball wants to join them."

I put my arms around her neck. She didn't shake me off but her mind was elsewhere. Mentally she was in the forest with that unknown pack, running down a deer, savoring an easy meal. Enjoying the company of the pack.

"Snowball misses her pack. She wants to be part of a family. The wolf pack outside is a family of sorts."

I hugged her harder. "We're her family."

The howls abated. The hunt took the pack elsewhere and Snowball's mind returned to the roaring fire and two people who loved her. "I'm scared." I looked to Buck for understanding. "What if some day she hears a pack of wolves and joins them? What if nothing we can do will bring her back?"

"All we can do is hope that doesn't happen. And watch her carefully. And don't leave her alone." He ran his tongue over his teeth. He didn't want to have to say what came next but he knew it was necessary. "You must understand that Snowball is a very large and efficient predator in a world where she doesn't belong."

"She belongs in Otherworld."

"The gateway is closed and may never reopen."

"I'd rather see her there than have her be killed here because she's chasing deer."

He wrapped both Snowball and myself in sturdy arms. "She's our responsibility now. If the gateway never opens again, we do what we can to give her a good life." We looked at each other grimly over the wolf pup's back.

The wolves didn't return. When the plow cleared the road the next day, we followed it to the center to make sure there'd been no damage. Then we parted,

Buck to give the lectures that had been cancelled because of the storm, me to take notes on the classes I'd missed. When the school day ended, he returned to his home and I to mine.

I bounced from one wall to another in frustration. The home I'd grown up in felt all wrong. Will and Jake didn't notice, nor did my father, but Mom did. "It's Buck, isn't it?" Home from work, she dropped her book bag on the table.

"What are you talking about?" I pretended to be interested in what books had been popular at the library, not a small thing in a town that had just endured a blizzard. The library was more popular in winter than in the summer, requiring longer hours. She was tired.

But she wasn't fooled. "Something happened, didn't it?"

"I stayed at his house and we took care of Snowball."

She dropped her coat on top of her books and went to find something for dinner. It wasn't necessary, I'd already started a hot dish. I busied myself in the kitchen and pretended there was nothing more to talk about. Again, she wasn't fooled.

All that evening and for many to follow, I felt her eyes as I went about my life. Then my dad also started watching me. And later, both Will and Jake did the same. But no one said anything. They were giving me the space to plot my own path through life though it was clear they thought they knew where that path led. Straight to Buck Porter.

Spring came and, with it, more problems with Snowball. Buck explained on one of my visits. "She wants to be outside all the time." After that I came as often as possible, often staying overnight. The family said nothing about my nights away and I was grateful for their tact. I told them that Snowball needed watching. They accepted my explanation and didn't laugh until they thought I couldn't hear.

As for Snowball, she was growing up. Our mind link was stronger than ever but the cute wolf pup was now almost a full grown wolf with a mind of her own. If she wanted to listen, she did, but just as often she ignored my wishes and did whatever she wanted.

As the weather warmed and the forest came alive, she exhilarated in the feel of wind on her body and in the myriad intoxicating scents of the woods in springtime. Tuned in to her emotions as I was, I knew what she was feeling so I knew that she remembered running slowly and with pain as a pup and I knew how important being able to run was to her now. The sheer joy was so piercing that I couldn't be angry, not even when she ran away.

I blamed myself. I hadn't been able to bring myself to call her back until it was too late, and she was out of sight. And out of my mind. I couldn't reach her mentally.

My stomach was in knots for hours as Buck and I searched the forest, calling until we were hoarse. I tried to locate her mentally but she'd learned to shut it off when she chose, which was whenever she wanted to do something she knew I wouldn't like. When she finally decided to come back of her own accord, we were limp with relief.

The next time she ran away, she chased a deer just for fun. Thankfully, she didn't kill it and when she was safely back at home she listened to my mental tirade without tuning me out. But she sulked all that day and into the night. I spent hours trying to get her to understand that she couldn't kill animals.

She couldn't understand why not. The pack killed, she remembered that from Otherworld. If they didn't kill, they didn't eat. It was difficult to make her understand that things were different now but, by the time morning rolled around, we'd made progress.

Buck was the expert on wolves. He gave me ideas that I channeled to Snowball until we were both exhausted. Snowball, on the other hand, had endless energy and loved the attention. Not until dawn did she wrap her tail around her nose and sleep the sleep of the innocent.

"I think I got it across to her that we don't kill animals for various reasons and that she shouldn't argue with her elders."

"That's a complicated concept."

"I put it simply. If I say she can kill it, she can. If I say not to kill it, she can't."

"It's a start."

"I'll work on the details later."

The sun rose. An entire night without sleep because of one recalcitrant wolf pup. We moved from the house to Buck's back yard, letting Snowball sleep in her favorite place, the braided rug by the fireplace. The outside world revived us somewhat. The grass was new, the day was spring warm, and sunshine poured extravagantly over everything. It was close to the end of the school year and Buck would be visiting his family in New York as soon as classed ended. I'd have Snowball at the farm while he was gone. I was there to work out the details.

We watched the wind riffle new lightly green leaves. "You graduate tomorrow." I nodded but said nothing. "What's next?"

"I haven't thought."

"If you move for a job somewhere else it'll complicate things."

"I'm not going anywhere."

"Your brand-new degree won't be all that useful in a small town."

"I'd rather pump gas than leave Snowball."

A scratching sound at the door said Snowball was awake and wanted out. After making a few circles of the yard she settled down and started digging a hole in Buck's yard. "So you're sticking around." After a moment, he added, "Good." Then he finished with, "I have to pack."

I graduated, had a wonderful party with friends I'd known all my life mingling with Buck and everyone else from the wolf center. The next day he dropped Snowball at the farm on his way to the airport.

She immediately took a tour of the farm to make sure everything was as she remembered. She paused for a long time at the sheep pen. I pretended not to notice how long she watched them. I also pretended not to notice how carefully my father watched her.

Two days into the visit I began to relax. Snowball hadn't shown any interest in the cattle other than to sniff the loafing shed on her way to the edge of the forest to do her business. She tarried longer by the sheep pen. When she was done, I led the way into the woods after snapping a leash on her in case she had a sudden yen to run away. But she was perfectly happy rediscovering her old haunts.

I kept her in the trees until I was sure my father wasn't around. Then I brought her to the sheep pen where I sat her down and let her know in no uncertain terms that these particular animals were not to be killed. That they were part of the farm. Part of the family, in a way. That they should be protected, not killed. She listened and seemed to understand, and I had to be content with that.

Three days into the visit things were going better than I'd have thought possible. I relaxed, even to rethinking my decision to let her live with Buck. Perhaps when he returned, I'd bring up the subject of letting her stay at the farm for a while.

The fourth day, I was mowing the grass while Snowball scampered around the yard and the sheep crowded against the fence because they didn't like the sound of the lawn mower. My dad had finished chores in the barn and was coming towards me when it happened.

The fence buckled beneath the combined weight of six sheep and collapsed. The sheep, finding themselves free, started to run towards the trees. My dad shouted and pointed towards them. I shut off the lawn mower and slid from the seat to help round them up, thinking as my feet hit the ground that there was no way either of us could reach the woods before the sheep got lost in the underbrush.

Snowball saw everything. She moved. She bared her teeth, a low growl emanating from her mouth and her ears flattening as she started after them. I stopped, frozen to the spot, frantically sending mental commands. *'Stop! Don't kill them!'* Over and over again, sending thoughts her way.

What I heard back was so unexpected that I doubled over in relief. *'Bad sheep. They belong in the pen.'*

As my father and I watched, Snowball covered the ground between herself and the sheep in the kind of flat-out run that could easily bring down a deer. Then she circled around them, growling and forcing them to bunch together until they stopped and milled about uncertainly. She put her nose to the ground and ran towards them in a zig-zag pattern. The sheep gave way as Snowball advanced, moving them inexorably back through the woods towards the broken place in the fence and then into the pen.

My dad quickly herded them into the barn and shut the door. Then he came to where I stood with Snowball. I was drained of energy. "I thought all along that she might have sheep dog in her. This proves it." He patted her on the head. "She can visit any time." He went to find lumber to repair the fence. But he gave Snowball a strange look as he disappeared in the barn.

As if there was more that he might have said. That he chose not to say.

I took Snowball for a walk in the forest where I dropped to the ground and hugged her for a long time before leaning against a tree.

Would she have rounded up the sheep if I hadn't been around or would she have killed them? I wished I knew the answer and hoped the day would never come when I'd find out.

I couldn't wait for Buck to return. I wanted to talk to him. I needed to talk to him. I needed him. I stared at light filtering through new, fuzzy leaves because I was in love with Dr Buck Portman, wolf researcher and recently promoted full college professor. In love with him in spite of myself. In love more than just wanting to be with him. To the extent of wanting to be with him for the rest of my life.

Yikes!

I rose, found Snowball, and walked her back to the house while wondering how my life had gotten so off track. I knew the answer, of course. My whole family knew the answer. It was about time I, too, admitted that two unexpected things had come along and changed my plans. The first thing was a wolf pup as large as a dire wolf and the other was a college professor the size of a pro fullback. Both larger than average, both more important than I'd have thought possible.

I didn't meet Buck at the airport because I didn't want him to know how important his return was to me. I didn't take Snowball to his place because I wanted her to stay with me. So it was a full week after his return before we saw each other. We finally met when he came to pick up Snowball.

"What happened while I was gone?" His head tilted, and he eyed me suspiciously.

"What do you mean?" At times he read me like a book. I hoped this wasn't one of those times.

"I know something happened. It had to have happened. I know Snowball so I know it did and, from the look on your face, I'm right. I'll get it out of you eventually so you might as well tell me now."

We were in the kitchen, which would normally be a poor place for confidences with everyone coming and going, but that day everyone was elsewhere. My parents were at a fertilizer workshop and the boys were taking a family fishing on the Delight. We had the room and the day to ourselves. So I told Buck what had happened.

He wasn't concerned. "She didn't attack them because she responded to your wishes. As a member of the pack, that's what she's supposed to do."

"What about the next time? I'm afraid of the future. I'm afraid for her."

"I am too." We were silent for a long time. "It's better for her to be at my place where there are fewer temptations."

"But there are wolves in the nearby forest."

There was nothing more to say so we stared at one another for what seemed like hours and was probably minutes. "You got a haircut while you were away."

"My mother's idea. She's afraid I'll become a long-haired hippy college professor."

"That'll never happen. You're not the type."

"Tell that to my family."

"If they are like my family, they won't listen."

Another long silence, until he said, in a hoarse voice, "I want a family." He sat up straighter and looked at the wall, the dust in the air, everywhere but at me. "Soon. Not soon. Now. I've been giving it a lot of thought."

"Got anyone in mind?" I flushed and wished for the hundredth time that I didn't blurt things out before thinking. But it was too late so I added, "Mia, maybe?

He snorted. "Mia? Never and you know it." His gaze darted everywhere and finally settled on me. "You." After a moment, he added, "If you're interested." And after another moment, "Which you are."

"What makes you so sure?"

"I know you."

A smile wound its way from somewhere inside of me to my lips. "Yes you do. I think you know me as well as you know Snowball."

An answering grin crossed his face, lighting up his eyes, pulling his eyebrows slightly together in a fruitless effort to erase the smile. "I know you better than Snowball." His grin turned smug. "I've been thinking about us ever since I left. I missed you, damn it! I missed you so much that, what with missing you and thinking about you and then thinking about us all the time I was with my parents, they finally informed that I was driving them crazy and asked who was the woman in my life."

"And?"

"I gave them your name. They wanted to see your picture."

"You don't have one."

"They let me know I'd better get one ASAP and shoot it off it to them. Oh, and they said to tell you they approve."

"Without seeing me?"

"They trust my judgment." He scooted closer. "They are nice that way." And still closer. "So what about it? Are we an item or not?"

"I thought we just settled that."

"Not wholly. Are we an item? Or are we engaged?" He might have heard my thoughts. "I want us to be engaged."

"Okay."

"Okay what?"

"Okay, we're engaged."

I expected the workshop on fertilizer to last all day. It should have lasted all day. It didn't. It was just past noon and at that moment my parents walked into the kitchen. I gave Buck credit. My dad can be a formidable person but Buck stood up and informed my parents that we were engaged. "Jane and I are getting married."

My dad just grunted and said something to the effect that it was about time. My mother rolled her eyes and hugged us both and offered the back yard for the wedding if we were interested. "I promise that the grass will be cut, the flower beds weeded, and the barn cleaned enough that it won't smell like a barn."

By the time Will and Jake returned from their charter with a fistful of cash and a stringer of walleyes for dinner, everything was settled. We would be married in the back yard in August. Buck's family would fly in and stay at the farm. It would be a simple ceremony.

Will considered the calendar that no longer had the first day of school circled because I'd graduated. He circled it now because in the future that day would become a part of my life and, by extension, of theirs. "August means you'll have time for a honeymoon before school begins."

Jake said, "We'll watch Snowball for you."

Chapter Fifteen

Details for the wedding were easy. What to do with Snowball was another story altogether. We appreciated Jake's offer but said we'd have to think about it. "Surely you won't take her with you." We looked at each other, then everywhere except at Jake. He whistled. "You're insane, both of you. No one takes a dog on a honeymoon."

My cell's ring saved us from having to answer. It was the clinic in town returning my question about a job. They wanted to interview me. "We have to go," I said hurriedly, and Buck and I almost ran to his truck.

I got the job and we sat around his house the rest of that day trying to come up with a plan for Snowball after the wedding. "I suppose it depends on where we go. We haven't talked about a honeymoon yet."

"I don't want to have to buy a whole lot of clothes that I'll never wear again." I stuck my booted foot out. "So I vote for someplace easy where we don't have to dress up and act nice."

"Like the island."

Shivers crept along my spine. He was saying what I'd been thinking. "The island that leads to Otherworld."

Our looks met. We knew where we would go. "It'll make perfect sense to anyone who asks. We'll be honeymooning where we met, on a remote, romantic island."

"As I recall, it was darned uncomfortable. We didn't make a fire because of the drought."

"There hasn't been a lot of rain this summer either so it'll be pretty dry this time too."

"Think the cave between worlds is open?"

"We can check and see. If it is we can visit Silver. Show her how Snowball is doing."

"We will go to the island but we'll actually honeymoon in Otherworld." Though we couldn't tell anyone, we'd know that we'd have the most amazing honeymoon possible, truly in another world. "We'll have to bring enough weapons to overpower anything that might try to eat us."

"My granddad left me a bunch of rifles and a couple pistols. We can hold off an army if we bring them all."

Everyone thought we were honeymooning on a romantic island and were bringing Snowball along so she could run without worrying about her. But, when no one was looking, we packed guns and plenty of ammunition in addition to all the camping gear we'd be able to backpack through a long cave. And we brought rubber boots in case we had to wade through the creek to reach Otherworld.

When we reached the island and then the cave, we were glad for the boots. The river was a small but steady stream. As we pulled them on, we inspected the river and the cave it flowed from. "A couple of well-placed sticks of dynamite would blow that pond to smithereens and the river would never again fill the cave completely."

"We could come and go as we please?"

"I think so. But we'd have to disguise the entrance."

"There are lots of bushes. We can pull them over the entrance. No one will see it unless they are looking for it."

We put the decision off until our return. Much would depend on what we found in Otherworld. The wolf pack might be gone forever.

Snowball didn't want to go wading. She hung back and whimpered when we called her. Only by picturing Silver in my mind and sending the picture to Snowball's mind did she finally come and, even then, she did so reluctantly. But once we were in the dark, she stuck close. Her ears flicked back and forth. We didn't know if she remembered her first trip through or not, but she paid close attention to every step, every turn, every sound that bounced from the rock walls.

We rested several times, but not for long. Our boots weren't insulated, and the cold water turned our feet to ice. I felt sorry for Snowball but her whimpering had ceased as soon as we were well into the cave. I decided that perhaps she did remember something. That at some level she might know where she was going. I became sure of it once we were close to Otherworld. She stopped a moment, listened, sniffed the air, and took off like a shot. We stumbled after her as best we could.

We stepped from the cave and into a remembered world of vastness and primeval forests. Of eagles larger than any in our world circling overhead and two deer grazing mere yards away that startled and took off with Snowball after them.

I started to call her back but Buck put out a hand to stop me. "This is her world, Jane. Let her go."

"We can't let her get into the habit of chasing deer."

"We can't stop her. Not here, not in this place."

I went quiet because he was right, though I knew re-training her when we returned home would be difficult.

We dropped to a large rock, perhaps the same one that Buck had stumbled over that had led to his broken arm. We just sat. It seemed a miracle that we'd made it through the cave. That we were in Otherworld.

Finally, Buck said, "We should get this show on the road. Get a camp set up." He grinned down at me. "I promise to help this time around."

"You're not a paying client anymore."

We set to work, but as we pounded in stakes or scooped water from the clear pond into our buckets, we were listening for Silver's wolf pack. But we heard nothing through all the hours of the day. And, yes, the days in Otherworld were longer than ours. We knew because we'd brought a battery-powered clock. But even with those extra hours, no wolves showed themselves.

We spent the night, the first of our married life, in

the tent, wrapped in sleeping bags and each other, with Snowball curled at our feet. "I'm glad she's here." I whispered to Buck because I didn't want to encourage her to join us. "She'll know if anything is sneaking around in the dark that wants to attack us."

"If she does, this will take care of it." Buck patted the pistol inches from our heads. He'd proved to be a crack shot at the shooting range in town. Better than me.

The night seemed to last forever but in reality was only a few hours longer than nights at home. In the morning we had pancakes and sausage cooked over a camp stove. Then we settled down to wait for the wolf pack.

"If they are still around."

"If they are still alive." Buck's concern was plain to see. "Wolves are apex predators but they still have a tough life."

"There might be new pups. Snowball is over a year old."

"We'll see when we meet them. If they are nearby." He touched my forehead. "Do you sense anything? Can you call Silver?"

"I've never tried except when she was close, but I'll see if I can sense her." I'd do anything to see my friend again. I closed my eyes and centered my thoughts. I cast them far and wide. Then I opened my eyes and said, in amazement, "I can see the whole area in my mind. It's really weird. I see what's beyond the hills and among the trees. I see everywhere."

Buck had spent a lot of time thinking about my

psychic connection to Snowball. He'd watched and listened and had developed some ideas about how it worked. By extension, the same should hold true for my connection to Silver. Now he thought he knew what was happening. "You're seeing through wolf eyes."

"Yes, I believe you're right. I see from a different perspective."

"The question is, are you seeing what Snowball remembers from when she was a pup and what Silver showed you when we were here before? Or are you seeing through Silver's eyes right now?"

My breath whooshed out. "I see what Silver sees. What she's looking at."

"Can you tell where they are?"

I shook my head. "I don't recognize the place so I don't know if she's close or not. I'll see if I can call her." I closed my eyes again and concentrated on Silver. I showed her Snowball. "If she sees Snowball all grown up and with her leg healed, it should tell her that she's seeing something that's happening right now instead of seeing a memory."

"Let's hope it works."

We waited. Snowball ran here and there, sniffing and getting reacquainted with her childhood home. Buck watched carefully. "She's not going near the den."

"I don't sense any pups, but that could be because none of this year's pups are psychic."

"Or that there aren't any this year. It happens sometimes."

As I tried to sort out the beauty that surrounded us from the picture in my mind, a movement in the trees caught our attention. At first we drew nearer to each other and Buck cocked the pistol, but, as the shape of wolves racing our way became clearer he put it down and we waved and shouted. The pack was coming, and Silver was leading the way.

"Glad to see you again." Silver sent me a sidewise glance as she closed in on her daughter, sniffed her all over and inspected her healed leg. *"It's right again. She can run."* And finally, *"You kept your promise. Thank you."*

"I wasn't sure we could return."

"I remember you saying that. I'm glad you're here."

"The river was low, we could wade through the cave."

Buck waited quietly until my friend and I were finished. Then he asked, "Did she mention new pups?"

The moment he mentioned new pups the image popped into my mind and Silver saw it. *"No pups this year. Not every year, not since Snowball and her brothers were born."* With that sly sense of humor I'd come to associate with her, she added, *"Quite enough wolves to feed as it is. The pack is the right size now."*

An uneasy feeling stole over me. *"Snowball has lived with people for a long time now. She doesn't know how to hunt."*

Silver came close and sat. I did the same and we faced each other. The rest of the pack and Buck moved away slightly to give us room. It was clear that something important was happening.

"Should she stay with you? Is that what you are saying?"

As I thought about Snowball staying in Otherworld, my stomach clenched. She was a part of me. Our psychic connection was unique and beautiful. But she was a native of this world, not of ours. *"I don't know. I'll be honest and tell you that it will be hard for her if she stays with us because she's different."*

"Are there no wolves where you live?"

"None like your pack. Our wolves are smaller. But if she stays here, she'll have to learn how to hunt all over again and she's already lost a full year's experience."

I explained that in our world if she killed prey she'd be punished so she'd learned not to chase and kill animals but to protect them. Silver thought that over. *"What does Snowball want?"*

Silver was a good mother. She wanted what was best for her child even if meant she'd never see her again. I was ashamed of wanting Snowball to stay with me for my own selfish reasons. But I was still concerned about her ability to hunt after a year away from the pack.

Silver understood my concern. *"If she stays, we'll help her as we would have helped her if her leg had never healed."*

I knew she spoke the truth. The pack cared for its members. They lived as one unit, they fought as one, and they made sure no one went hungry. With her leg healed Snowball would be better off than if she'd stayed in Otherworld with a bad leg even though she had a lot of catching up to do. She was healthy and strong and could run like the wind.

"She'll have to decide for herself."

I told Buck the result of our talk. He put one arm around my shoulder. "I know how hard it'll be for you if she stays here."

"She must decide her own future."

Silver and I both bent our minds towards Snowball. Both of us sent the same thought to her. That she could live with the pack or with me. That it was her choice. Then we broke contact with her mind because we didn't want to influence her decision. We wanted to know that, whatever she decided, it would be her choice and hers alone.

Then we waited. The pack watched because even though they didn't know what was going on, they knew something important was about to happen. Buck kept that arm around me in moral support but he said nothing because there was nothing to say.

It was all up to Snowball.

She came towards us and sniffed Buck and me. She curled around our legs and asked to be petted and cuddled. We thought she'd decided to come home with us. But then she moved towards the pack and Silver, whining and sniffing each member of the wolf pack she'd been born into. She gave special attention to her brothers, Uno and Dos. The three of them ended up chasing each other around and around for a good two minutes.

Then she stopped still. She went to the space

between our campsite and the pack and she simply sat there and looked from one to the other.

Then she ran full bore towards Buck and I and jumped up on us to give us a huge, furry, wolf hug. Then she went to join the pack.

She had made her decision. She would remain in Otherworld.

It was a long time before I could open my mind to anything because I didn't want Silver or Snowball to know I was crying. Silver's thoughts came to me clear and with full understanding of my feelings. *"Visit us again. Often."*

"We will. As often as we can." I turned to Buck. "You said we can lower the water level in the cave so we can come whenever we want, even in rainy years."

"I'm pretty sure it can be done."

"Then we'll do it because I don't know if I can face never seeing Snowball or Silver again."

"We'll do it. We'll keep the doorway between worlds open." Then, prosaic and practical as ever, he added, "But make sure Silver understands that it's not a good idea for wolves from this world to visit ours. It could be dangerous."

I passed on to Silver everything Buck had said. She said she understood and that the pack would never enter the cave again. And she added one last time that she hoped we'd visit often.

We planned on sleeping in the tent that night but it didn't happen. Instead, we dragged our sleeping bags and air mattresses outside and slept beneath those strange stars among a pile of dire wolves. Snowball slept curled between Buck and me and Silver was nearby. All night long thoughts drifted from Snowball to Silver to me, then back again. I don't think I slept at all. But by morning, we'd said everything we had to say to each other and I was ready to return without Snowball.

The trip back through the cave was without incident. Once through, we spent many hours staring out at Lake of the Woods thinking up a story to explain Snowball's disappearance.

"Her original owner hadn't abandoned her after all, but instead has been returning to the island ever since in the hope of finding her. Their reunion was so heartwarming that we had to let her go with him." Buck's arm curved around me as his words were lofted across the water by a momentary breeze.

"I wouldn't believe such a ridiculous story." I welcomed his closeness.

"Doesn't matter if anyone believes it. It's only important that they can't dispute it."

"We can say we didn't get the owner's name or where he lives."

"So they can't check it out."

I sighed. "I guess it'll do." I curled into my new husband and said what I was really feeling. "I miss Snowball. I didn't realize how much a part of my life she was."

"I know." I started to say that he couldn't know, no one could, but I checked myself because, if anyone on earth could understand what I was feeling, it was Buck. He cleared his throat and said, "I know I can't replace

Snowball."

"Of course you can't and you shouldn't. You're not Snowball, you're Buck Portman."

"I wish there was something I could do."

"You already are."

"I'm not doing anything."

I turned into his shoulder. "Yes you are, just by listening." His arm grew tighter around my shoulders and some of the hurting lessened.

During the week on the island, the hurting became bearable. Buck inspected what would be a pool during wet years that would prevent us from returning to Otherworld. "I don't think it'll be a big project to blow that wall to smithereens. It'll be gone next week."

I smiled and discovered that Buck was already growing larger and Snowball smaller in my mind. When we piled our things on the Delight for the trip home, I couldn't imagine not living without him and I was able to think of Snowball in Otherworld without becoming depressed.

We told our concocted story when we got home. We didn't know if the people at the wolf center believed us. My family didn't. The first time I was alone with my dad after telling the story, he said in that quiet way he has, "I know there's more to it than what you said and I'll not ask. I'll trust you. But maybe someday you'll tell me what really happened and how a very unusual monster wolf pup ended up living with us for a few months."

I looked him in the eye. "It's complicated. I hope that some day we can tell you everything. But I warn you that you won't believe it." He nodded and never mentioned Snowball again other than to say she'd done an excellent job of herding the sheep when they got out of their pen.

Then I went home with Buck and set about learning how to be Jane Porter. It was easier than expected and at the same time it was harder. The forest beyond our back yard was large and mysterious and we were close enough to the center for the howls of wolves to drift to us on the waning evening wind.

Every time those howls drifted towards me, I remembered Silver and Snowball and the rest of the pack and my thoughts would turn to Otherworld. At such times, Buck would take one look at me and lead me to the window or outside and together we'd listen to the wind and the wolves and speculate about Otherworld and how Snowball and the pack were doing. And wonder at the strange psychic link I had to both Silver and Snowball. Then we'd go inside and Buck would make sure to distract me, which was ridiculously easy. He's a real hunk.

Epilogue

The summer had been rainy but ever since Buck dynamited the pool weather didn't matter. We could come and go as we wished but we only did so once a year in order not to arouse suspicion. August was a good month, before school started and our lives got busy with other things.

It was a good time for Buck to update his research on the dire wolf pack. He said that, along with the insights my psychic link provided, the dire wolf pack helped him understand wolves in our world. It must have been true because he's gaining a reputation as a young but respected wolf researcher. So on a chosen week in the middle of August, we packed our things, powered up the Delight, and set off for the island we now knew well.

Before entering the cave to Otherworld we used branches to sweep away our tracks and when we were done we pulled branches over the opening. No one would find the cave by following our tracks but, just in case we missed a track or two and they found it, we'd piled rocks in the back of that first room so it wouldn't look like the cave went any farther. All a casual observer would see was the creek coming from what appeared to be solid rock and the water was so cold anyone would think twice before wading in it.

Satisfied with our work concealing the path to Otherworld, we made the trek through the cave. We carried cameras to record things we'd never show anyone and sleeping bags and air mattresses. We didn't need a tent because the last time we'd visited we'd made a rough log cabin near the Otherworld end of the cave.

When we emerged into the long, sun filled days of Otherworld, we dropped our packs to the ground and simply took in the sights and smells of a place we'd come to love. There were far too many large animals that would like to eat us to be completely comfortable but we felt safe in the cabin with its solid log walls.

When we built it the wolf pack inspected it minutely, sniffing the fresh-cut logs and peeing around the outside to mark it as belonging to them. And us. We felt honored.

Now, in the warm sunshine, we leaned back against a boulder and closed our eyes and I sent my thoughts outward in search of Silver and Snowball and the other wolves that had been born since Snowball with whom I could link mentally. Three of them posses that wonderful trait.

I wish I knew how it works, I wish I knew how to study psychic phenomena but I don't and I don't dare ask too many questions. So I just accept it.

When my mental call was answered, we rose to wait for the pack to arrive. First over the hill was a magnificent, white dire wolf. Snowball came as fast as she could run and just about knocked us over with her enthusiastic greeting. Silver followed, older and slower but still the alpha wolf. The queen.

The rest of the pack followed and soon we were surrounded by dire wolves from another world. And we all settled down to the business of catching up on everything that had happened since our last visit

THE END

Don't miss the first book in the Legend Series, Spirit Legend.

PROLOGUE

It didn't have fins and a tail or fur or even a hard shell like the other inhabitants of the lake. Neither did it swim like those other inhabitants did. Fish. Turtles. The occasional otter and, of course, the beavers. It liked the beavers.

Instead of swimming, it flowed, following the moving water and becoming one with it because it was so easy and it liked the feeling of being a part of the lake. It didn't need to become water but the sensation was pleasurable.

It played a bit, turning all the colors of the rainbow and more and rising above the surface briefly for a look around. While it turned and twisted in the air, it sang because it liked the sound. Music was something it had learned since coming to this place. It liked music.

It also liked the forest and the tiny lake behind the beaver dam, the place it chose to live. The lake was just the right size. Not too large and not too small. The water had been cold when it first arrived but that had been easily remedied. Most of all, it liked the solitude of the isolated area and the silence because, in that silence it could sing as much as it wished and flaunt the colors it knew how to create. It was beautiful, and it sang lovely songs even though no one watched or listened. It didn't mind not having an audience, though watchers and listeners would be nice on occasion.

It was alone but it was never lonely. It didn't understand the concept of loneliness because, being the only one of its kind, how could it miss another? But it did enjoy the occasional visitors that passed through the area. Deer came now and then to drink in the lake. Sometimes bears passed by. And once in a while people came. People were interesting. Different. It was curious about people. People had taught it about music.

It had stayed as long as it had in this particular place because of its curiosity and because of the people. There was much to learn here and it liked to learn. It liked that more than singing, more than joining with the water, more than turning all the colors of a rainbow, more even than watching the change of the seasons and the years.

It was curious about everything. The animals, the plants, the wind soughing through the trees. Most of all, though, it wondered about the people. They came in silent canoes and they played flutes. No other living things in this place had either of those things.

Canoes indicated intelligence and technology. So when people came sometimes it would come close and look them over and call out to them. But they never answered. It couldn't understand why not but thought that someday it might know the reason.

Don't miss the first book Spirit Legend. Read the first chapter here.

PROLOGUE

It didn't have fins and a tail or fur or even a hard shell like the other inhabitants of the lake. Neither did it swim like those other inhabitants did. Fish. Turtles. The occasional otter and, of course, the beavers. It liked the beavers.

Instead of swimming, it flowed, following the moving water and becoming one with it because it was so easy and it liked the feeling of being a part of the lake. It didn't need to become water but the sensation was pleasurable.

It played a bit, turning all the colors of the rainbow and more and rising above the surface briefly for a look around. While it turned and twisted in the air, it sang because it liked the sound. Music was something it had learned since coming to this place. It liked music.

It also liked the forest and the tiny lake behind the beaver dam, the place it chose to live. The lake was just the right size. Not too large and not too small. The water had been cold when it first arrived but that had been easily remedied. Most of all, it liked the solitude of the isolated area and the silence because, in that silence it could sing as much as it wished and flaunt the colors it knew how to create. It was beautiful, and it sang lovely songs even though no one watched or listened. It didn't mind not having an audience, though watchers and listeners would be nice on occasion.

It was alone but it was never lonely. It didn't understand the concept of loneliness because, being the only one of its kind, how could it miss another? But it did enjoy the occasional visitors that passed through the area. Deer came now and then to drink in the lake. Sometimes bears passed by. And once in a while people came. People were interesting. Different. It was curious about people. People had taught it about music.

It had stayed as long as it had in this particular place because of its curiosity and because of the people. There was much to learn here and it liked to learn. It liked that more than singing, more than joining with the water, more than turning all the colors of a rainbow, more even than watching the change of the seasons and the years.

It was curious about everything. The animals, the plants, the wind soughing through the trees. Most of all, though, it wondered about the people. They came in silent canoes and they played flutes. No other living things in this place had either of those things.

Canoes indicated intelligence and technology. So when people came sometimes it would come close and look them over and call out to them. But they never answered. It couldn't understand why not but thought that someday it might know the reason.

CHAPTER ONE

THE FIRST EVENING

The aerial photos covered most of the two pushed-together tables. The corners and edges were carefully matched to create one large picture, green being the predominant color. Green as in an evergreen forest. The only things breaking the green were a few darker lines representing creeks that crisscrossed the area, a fire trail or logging road or two circling the outer edges, and, in the center of it all, a small area of blue that could be a tiny lake, a pond, or, more likely, a swamp.

After scooping up our empty glasses and replacing them with additional drinks on a third table pulled close, Mickey of Mickey's Pub and Eatery leaned over the photos and perused them casually. Then again, only this time not so casually. In detail. Then he thoughtfully traced one of the creeks with a finger. "I took a canoe along this creek once when I was a kid." The finger jabbed at the blue in the center of the montage. "And I ran across this lake. It was shallow, lots of rice beds along the shore. I figured I'd come back and harvest the rice when it was ripe. I wanted a Harley in the worst way and Harleys are expensive but rice brought a good price that year so I thought I might be able to buy a used one."

There was a huge motorcycle in Mickey's garage. "So

that's when you got your Harley?"

"Nope. I didn't go back and harvest that rice." Something about his voice gave me pause as I followed his finger.

I didn't look at the man across the table from me. In fact, I avoided him. My boss, Ian Macallister, owner and CEO of Macallister Outdoors. According to scuttlebutt, he was both knowledgeable and competent and he missed nothing. No one knew why he decided to visit the corporate retreat in Johns Falls. Rumors abounded.

I squirmed inwardly, forced my expression to be blank, and concentrated even harder on the photos so he wouldn't know I was intentionally ignoring him, though my stomach churned as I tried to decipher just how angry he was. That anger was my fault.

The Johns Falls airport was too small to have a waiting room or any of the luxuries of larger airports so Ian Macallister was waiting on a folding chair hastily provided by the single airport employee. He was polite enough when I peeled into the parking lot, ran full bore into the waiting room and skidded to a stop in front of him when I arrived. The only Macallister Outdoors employee not busily preparing for the Big Boss' arrival. Bad choice, they should have known better than to ask me to pick him up and tote him back to the Center. But they were desperate.

With the result that, in the airport, when I pulled up in front of him with a smile pasted on my face and a rumpled Macallister Outdoors shirt on, his back wasn't touching the chair. Such posture could indicate anger... or frustration... or merely that he was a fitness freak and always bore himself with a ramrod straight back. I hoped it was the last but, figuring it was more likely the first, I waited to be fired, smiling weakly and standing tall so as to present as imposing a figure as I knew how.

His expression didn't change. I felt myself shrinking as he unfolded from the airport chair and loomed over me, forcing me to look up into his six foot something self. Into his eyes. They were dark. From anger? Or were they always midnight blue so the color didn't necessarily mean I'd soon be unemployed? Was he born with bottomless eyes? I hoped so but doubted that was the case.

I had to fight my inner fear in order not to fold my arms across my body in a feeble attempt to ward off his anger. But he said nothing, merely picked up the single suitcase that was his luggage and asked if there was somewhere in town where he could eat since it was getting late. My fault again, having made him wait through the normal dinner hour. The only Macallister Outdoors employee without an internal clock. How was I to know it was so late?

A gust of wind rattled the terminal window. I glanced outside. My shoulders slumped. The storm that had pushed his flight up a couple hours was hitting in all the fury the weather forecast had predicted and then some. I'd seen the clouds as I ran across the parking lot and would have liked to stop in awe of the fury that was about to dump on me if I didn't hurry inside. Rain so hard I'd be transporting my boss to the Center through the kind of downpour that would require headlights and four-wheel drive. But I hadn't stopped to admire the storm, I'd just gone inside and slammed the door behind me.

In the airport, the Big Boss waited for an answer. He wanted to know where he could eat dinner. I forced myself to breathe in and out, in and out, until I could speak normally, and suggested Mickey's Pub and Eatery. Then I followed him out of the terminal and into the storm where I learned that the threat of rain before I entered the airport was fulfilled a hundred-fold when we left.

There was no waiting for the storm to pass, no chance it

would blow over while we ate. It was supposed to last all night. Storms threatened to hammer the area off and on for the next couple weeks with one storm following another as if they were trains on the same track, with possibly a day or two in between.

So I'd followed my boss through the airport door, stepped into the rain and wind and was almost knocked sidewise. Ian Macallister, however, taller and strong as an ox, was a rock. I'd moved closer to use his body as a windbreak, never mind that he was building up to fire me. Until then, I'd bask in the relative calm his bulk provided. Still, as I let the wind pound him instead of me, I decided not to mention the real reason for my tardiness until he was in a more mellow frame of mind than rain and wind provided.

Mickey brought still another round of complementary drinks. Strong, I'd guess, knowing Mickey. I didn't drink because it was my job to drive my boss to the Center and Mickey knew that, so mine were Virgin Mary's. Ian Macallister's weren't.

The plan was that when Mickey's drinks had my boss in a mellow frame of mind, I would explain my late arrival. Until then I threw Mickey a grateful look and he nodded imperceptibly in answer. He knows me, Mickey does, and the endless rounds of drinks were a gesture of true friendship.

I looked again at the photos, wondering what about them was so seductive. They were just photos of the property the Center had recently acquired, and they showed miles of unspoiled wilderness. Still, I'd felt a shiver run over me after I printed them out and put them together to form a comprehensive picture. I'd found myself staring at a pine and hardwood forest. A jewel, a rare and ecologically unique acquisition to be cared for with love.

That had to be the reason it got to me so thoroughly. Sent shivers along my spine. It was unique, that had to be why I felt it through my whole being. Nothing else made sense. Even in Mickey's Eatery, looking at photos I'd seen before sent a shiver along my spine. And, as the Center's newest forester, I'd be doing the caring.

I'd been so enthralled that I'd forgot the time, nothing new for me, and that was why I was late, though I doubted my boss would see that as a good reason to leave him cooling his heels on a folding chair. Now, if silence was any indication, I'd not work for Macallister Outdoors much longer. Not long enough to visit the rare slice of wilderness that had caused my lateness.

In the rough log and fireplace ambiance of Mickey's Pub and Eatery, Ian Macallister moved for the first time since finishing dinner. My breath stopped but all he did was lean closer to follow Mickey's pointing finger as it jabbed at the map. "You say you've been there?" Mickey nodded. "And you intended to return?" Mickey nodded again. "But you didn't?" Mickey shook his head and my boss asked quietly, with no inflection, "Why not?"

Mickey was glad to talk. He's a loquacious guy. "When my parents found out where I'd been, they were angry." Mickey moved the empty glass from one hand to the other, restlessly. "No, they weren't angry, that's the wrong word. They were concerned. No, that's not right either. They were… scared."

I peered at the photos. There was nothing dangerous about the property Macallister Outdoors had purchased. No cliffs, no dangerous rapids in any of the several creeks, nothing that I could see. Then I thought of a possible reason. "Was the bottom of the lake mud? If you were alone and overturned your canoe, you'd not have made it to shore."

He shook his head. "It did look muddy when I was there, but that wasn't the reason."

Ian's lips pursed, and he zeroed in on Mickey. "Then why didn't they let you go back?"

"Because of the,... thing... in the lake."

I examined the tiny blue area that could be a lake. Or a pond. Or a swamp. "It's a wide area of a creek is all. Nothing unusual about it. Nothing in it." No islands, no large boulders thrusting upwards to trip unwary boaters. "It's hardly a lake at all."

"The creek backs up behind a beaver dam. It forms a small lake but if that dam breaks, the lake will cease to exist."

"It doesn't look dangerous."

"It's not the lake itself that scared them."

Ian peered closer. "Then what?"

Mickey curled his shoulders forward the way people do when they are embarrassed. "It was because of the spirit that lives in the lake. Or spirits. No one knows if it's one spirit or a lot of them."

"Spirit?" I laughed, an explosion of sound that released some of my pent-up tension. "Really?" His parents were Chippewa and their ancestors had lived in the area forever, but his dad was a banker and his mom operated a jewelry store. They were educated, savvy people. "Your mom and dad don't believe that stuff."

"You know them. Of course they don't. But that one time, they did. Or at least they believed what their parents had told them enough to not want to take any chances."

"Your grandparents believed in spirits?" I'd met his grandparents. They both had college degrees. "How far back does this go? Who started this fantasy?"

"I don't know. A long time. Hundreds of years, maybe. Probably."

"And you believe it?"

"I didn't say I believe it. I said my folks wouldn't let me go back to harvest wild rice so I had to get a job in town to earn money for my first bike. And it wasn't a Harley, either, and it would have been if I'd got that wild rice and sold it. I couldn't afford a Harley until years later."

Ian Macallister leaned back, a half smile giving his face expression for the first time since I saw him in the airport terminal. He still said nothing, choosing to listen, but I was sure he heard every word, saw every expression, and correctly interpreted every nuance. As the rumors about him predicted, and I now knew those rumors were true. The man didn't miss a thing.

For some reason, the topic of spirits interested him. Mellowed him. Maybe enough to forget to fire me. So I talked about spirits. "What is this spirit supposed to be like?

"Or spirits. Plural, maybe. Or singular. Nice sometimes. Other times, not so nice. Depends."

"On what?"

"The old people... my grandparents and the people before them... didn't say. Just that whatever is in that lake...
"

"It's not a true lake, just a wide spot in a river," Ian interjected in a low voice.

"Whatever is in the lake doesn't suffer fools gladly. Or is reclusive. Or afraid. That's the best way I can put it." Mickey was uncomfortable beneath my boss' scrutiny. Ian Macallister's eyes were darker than before and intense. Because, unlike Mickey, he believed in ghosts? "According to the old people, it depends on who is at the lake and what they do." He stopped tossing the glass from hand to hand and that broke the spell his words had cast over me. "All I can say is it didn't talk to me and, while I was there I didn't see anything resembling a spirit. Maybe because there's no such thing."

"Most likely that's it." Ian wanted to ask more but Mickey moved away, glass in hand.

"Have you ever heard the wind in the trees?" I yelled after him, making sure the topic of ghosts stayed in the forefront of the conversation because my continued employment might depend on it. "Some people think it sounds like voices. Like someone singing."

Mickey paused in his headlong rush, the picture of injured dignity. "My people have lived in the forest for hundreds of years. I think they know the sound the wind makes well enough not to mistake it for anything other than what it is. The wind." He continued on and disappeared into the kitchen.

"Or the sound of water on rocks," I continued, turning to Ian Macallister and adding to the list of possibilities in order to mellow him more. "Or an echo if the creek has steep enough banks."

"Or everything you mentioned." He pulled his chair closer to the photos and leaned over them, effectively shutting me up. "This talk of spirits and beaver dams and lakes and rivers makes me curious." He gathered the photos into a pile that he then stuffed into the large envelope I'd carried from the Explorer when we arrived. "I'd not given any real thought to this new acquisition when I flew in today. My plans were more along the lines of bookkeeping. But I'm thinking about changing them."

"To what?"

"Checking out the new property. The wilderness. Everything. All of it."

He didn't fool me. It was the lake that held his interest. And the spirit that legend said inhabited it. "Will you go alone?"

"I'll want a guide. I'm sure there's someone at the

Center whose job includes knowing their way around the property."

"A forester."

His eyebrows rose. "We employ foresters?"

It was hard to breathe. "Yes you do. Me. I'm the forester." Something told me that it was time to come clean. To tell the truth. "And that's why I was late. Because I was looking over the photos of the new property." I counted to ten until I could speak again and without the squeak that had made his eyebrows rise a bit. "I'm sorry for that."

He blinked. Tilted his head slightly. Let his eyebrows fall back to their normal position above his eyes. Frowned a second then let a smile slide briefly across what seconds earlier had been a chiseled countenance, and some of the fear that had almost immobilized me melted. "You were late? I hadn't noticed."

He was a nice liar. He had noticed, the chill in the airport had been enough to freeze the entire county, but he wanted to see the tiny lake in the forest and that meant he needed me. And that meant I'd keep my job and he'd be nice to me, at least until he'd seen everything he wanted to see.

The melting in my inner self continued and spread until I could breathe normally. He continued. "Can you take me tomorrow? I can't stay indefinitely and there are other things that need my attention while I'm here."

"The rain should let up by morning. It'll start again in a day or so, though. So tomorrow may be the only decent day to go." I checked the clock behind the bar. "It's late now and it'll be a long day tomorrow. We'll have to take four-wheelers for the last part of the trip to the lake. So we'd best get going soon if we want to get any sleep at all tonight. And we should be rested when we start off in the morning, it'll be a tiring journey."

"It's a long drive to the Center and the weather is lousy. How long will it take us to get there in this rain? Minutes? Hours?"

"Two hours at least. More if the road is muddy and we have to go slow."

He didn't like that. "That'll cut into tonight's sleep." He checked the rain hitting the windows with enough force to break any glass except the best. "What if we stay in town tonight? That way we'll get a good night's sleep and can still get started early. It'll be faster driving to the Center in the daylight and the rain will have stopped by then, won't it?"

I agreed that staying overnight was a good idea and he waved to Mickey, who'd returned to his bartending. "Is there a decent motel nearby?"

Mickey doesn't have a dirty mind but I made sure to explain why we wanted a motel. When he understood our reason for staying in town, he made a call and booked two rooms. "Height of the tourist season. Not many rooms left." He pointed out the window to a large building across the parking lot. "It's close. You don't even have to drive."

So, having dried out in front of Mickey's fireplace after our soggy arrival at the Pub, we went back into the driving rain and wind. The storm had grown fiercer. In seconds we were as wet as if we'd jumped into a nearby lake except with the addition of twigs and leaves stuck to our bodies. I ducked behind Ian Macallister again and hoped he didn't know I was using him as a buffer against the flying debris. But of course he did.

The motel receptionist stared at us in dismay as we dripped all over her pristine carpet. She pointed down a long hallway and said something about the last two rooms. "Not our biggest or most elegant but they are all we have left. We recently remodeled them. New beds. King size."

She added that they were across from each other. As we trudged towards the hallway, leaving wet footprints in the carpet and twigs and leaves everywhere, she breathed in distaste.

"I thought for a moment she wouldn't let us stay." Ian's sotto voiced words were dripping with sarcasm.

"Do we look that bad?"

He paused to give me a once-over and I had to look at him, too. "Yes we do." We resembled drowned rats.

Ian Macallister, I decided, was one of those people who looked good in any situation so I couldn't say he looked like a drowned anything. I wasn't so lucky. And I was dripping dirt as well as rainwater because I'd been in the woods before coming to town to pick him up. Which meant that, in the morning, though my clothes would be dry, they'd still be dirty. It wasn't fair. Before I could stop myself I blurted out, "You, at least, can change into something clean."

He stopped. "I'm sorry. I didn't think. I have my luggage with me but you don't have anything to change into." He turned back towards the receptionist. "Perhaps they can suggest a store where you can get something to wear."

I stopped him with a hand on his sopping wet sleeve. "Don't bother. It's too late, all the stores are closed." His eyebrows rose in question. "This is a small town. We don't believe in late hours."

"Surely there's something we can do about those wet things you are wearing." He looked about. "Perhaps there's a laundry?"

Was he insane? "And what will I wear while my clothes go round and round? I don't think nudity is allowed."

"Sorry." A frank grin spread across his face, changing him completely. He didn't laugh out loud but it was hard for him not to as I tried and failed to keep my face from turning red. "Tell you what. I'll do the laundry. You can wrap yourself in a towel and wait in your room in comfort while I watch the washer do its thing." The grin spread until, realizing it could be interpreted many ways, it disappeared as quickly as it had come. But it stayed in his eyes and, yes, they must always be the color of dark fire because he wasn't angry now, instead he was laughing at me, and they were still midnight eyes. "Afterwards, we can get some sleep."

I didn't want to stand in front of my boss dressed in a motel towel but I couldn't see any other option so I nodded and tried for nonchalance as he found our rooms. He slid his key card into the slot in his door. "I'll shower and change, and then I'll come for your things. Give me a half hour or so, that'll give you time to shower too." He looked me up and down, that flash of silent laughter lingering in the back of his eyes. "I hope half an hour will be enough." And, ducking in case I wanted to hit him, he disappeared inside, which made me wonder whether the big boss of Macallister Outdoors was possibly a nice guy after all.

Getting out of my wet clothes was such a relief it was almost erotic and standing in a spray of hot water was even more so. I used my fingers and the motel dryer to turn my hair into some semblance of order, almost wishing I'd given up long hair in favor of a cropped look, then deciding for the thousandth time, that braids are more practical most of the time and don't require frequent visits to a hair salon. Anyway, normally I wore a hat in inclement weather. This was an unexpected situation. I hadn't planned on a trip to town. So, instead of reaching for a pair of scissors, I redoubled my efforts.

The knock was loud enough that I had to assume there'd been several before that I hadn't heard because of the dryer noise. I grabbed the largest towel from the available pile and wrapped it around me as I went to answer what was now heavy pounding on the door. "Are you there? Are you okay?"

I opened it and peeked around. "I'm fine."

"It took you so long to answer I was concerned." One hand held his dripping clothes, the other a small box of detergent.

"Sorry." He stared at me in consternation. Stared at my hair. So I should have opted for a short style after all. He stared so hard that I unconsciously raked it with the hand that wasn't holding the towel in place. "I'll get my clothes."

"Okay." But his gaze didn't move from my hair. Until it slid downwards, then, realizing that he was looking me over when I was half-naked, it stopped and returned to my hair. Given its disheveled appearance, I'd rather he kept going, all the way down me and then up again. Better than the amazed expression, almost awe, that he couldn't hide as he inspected my hair again. That stare kept me rooted, unable to move. Until, flushing, he said, "I'll wait out here," and closed the door in my face.

What did he expect me to do with no hairbrush handy? What did he expect any normal human being to do when confronted with a rat's nest that hung half-way down a back and was messy to begin with, courtesy of being outdoors a lot, and probably worse now, thanks to the debris that had battered us both?

I tripped on my way to the bathroom to retrieve my clothes. And again on my way back. Looked to see what I'd tripped over and the carpet was smooth and unbroken which meant being face to face with my boss when he was newly clean and dressed and I was in a motel towel was getting to me.

I stopped and breathed deeply a few times before opening the door in order to thrust my wet, drippy clothes at him. Found myself inches from my boss. Backed off a bit and held the wet clothes near his middle. Mumbled thanks in his general direction and pulled the towel tighter around my middle, holding it with two hands now that they were both free.

As for the owner of Macallister Outdoors, he mumbled something in return and backed away while his face flushed cherry red and his gaze wandered freely over all of my towel-wrapped self as if he'd rather be doing anything other than what he was doing but couldn't help himself.

Good! I wasn't the only one who was embarrassed, and that knowledge gave me the courage to speak after clearing my throat a couple times and taking one last deep breath. "I'll be waiting." I closed the door, slumped against it and wished I'd not been late in picking up my boss because if I'd been punctual, there'd have been time to drive him back to the Center and I'd be home now watching reruns on TV.

When he knocked on my door a good hour later, I wasn't watching reruns. Instead, I was checking the weather. I snugged the towel tightly around me and opened the door with bated breath, wondering what part of me he'd stare at this time.

No part at all. His gaze went straight to the TV. "Looks bad for tomorrow."

My breath came and went normally because he was looking elsewhere and I even relaxed my hold on the towel slightly. "Not too bad. The storms will return, perhaps by evening, but during the day it should be decent. Sunny and warm."

"Then so as long as we get an early start and don't take too long checking out the new property, we should be okay?"

I nodded. "I'll pack ponchos just in case, but we should be back before any clouds gather." I didn't add that was a good thing because the land we'd be inspecting was rough and not a good place to be in a storm but I was so eager to see it myself that I didn't want to say anything that might cause him to cancel the trip.

As he handed me a neatly folded pile of dry clothes, my cell rang. So instead of taking my clothes, I hitched up the towel with one hand and grabbed the phone with the other. "Yes?" I wanted to kill whoever had the nerve to call with me in a delicate state of semi-nudity.

The Center was checking on the welfare of the big boss. "He's okay. He's here with me as a matter of fact." Talking about Ian, I found my gaze moving over him much as his had over me. Six feet at least since he was a good head taller than me, I already knew that, with dark eyes, I already knew that too, and dark brown hair that wouldn't accept taming over the lithe build of a person of athletic bent who could double as a model. Which I realized he did as I recalled some of the Macallister Outdoors clothing ads. If what I'd been told was true, the man could climb a mountain with the best of them and pose at the summit for a clothing ad.

Right now, he was mouthing a question. "Is that for me?"

I shook my head. Then I changed my mind and nodded because, though the Center had called me, he was the reason for the call. I mouthed back, "They are concerned."

He shut the door behind him with a well-aimed kick and, after a look to ask permission, took the cell from my hand. "This is Ian Macallister." A different voice from the one I'd heard thus far. The voice of command. Of the owner of Macallister Outdoors.

I wanted to beat a retreat to the bathroom to dress but my clothes were held tightly in his free hand. I was sure he'd forgotten them but his brows were knit in such concentration that I didn't dare take them. So I tried to make myself relax, an almost impossible task in a bath towel but somehow I managed. Sort of. Then I crawled onto the bed because the room was too small for any other furniture, tucked my feet beneath me and tried to look as if I did this every day.

The owner of Macallister Outdoors paced. Three feet one way, then three feet back, using all of the space the room afforded. He talked for a long time with the manager of the Center. Assured him we were both all right and had chosen to stay in town because of the weather. Informed him that early the next morning we'd need whatever was necessary to explore the new property. And handed me the phone. "He wants to know what to have ready."

Given that I couldn't hold the towel with both hands and talk too, I dropped one hand and stuck my feet straight out in front of me and took the phone to give what I hoped were crisp, professional instructions to have the four-wheel-drive truck ready with two four-wheelers in tow with the pack that I kept in my office for just such expeditions tied securely to one of them.

I was about to hang up when Ian waved to me that he wanted to talk again. When he took the phone, he said crisply, "Have the cook prepare breakfast for us. Make it hearty. We might be out a long time." He flipped the phone shut and handed it to me. I took it without dropping the towel, a rather neat trick, set it on the bed, there being no place else to put it, and waited for him to leave.

Instead he said, "Want some coffee?" He rubbed the back of his neck. "I don't know about you but I had enough liquor this evening to last a long time. I'd like to sober up a bit before going to bed so I'll hopefully wake up ready to go."

"Good idea." He waited so I asked, "Do you want me to make it?" Looking towards the complimentary coffee pot and grounds next to the sink.

"Would you?" Then he did a double take as I tried to move and couldn't without dropping the towel a bit. He turned even redder than earlier. "Sorry." He handed me my clothes. "I'll make coffee while you change." After a moment, he added, "Will you leave your cell here? I forgot a couple things I should mention to whomever is on duty at the Center." I handed him the cell and scooted to the bathroom as he headed for the coffee pot, cell in hand, having forgotten I existed.

By the time I returned from the bathroom once more wearing dry clothes that covered all of me except my feet because my boots were drying by the heater, he'd procured a travel hairbrush from the motel receptionist in addition to making coffee. "She said not to bother returning it."

"Probably afraid what she'd find in it."

"Your hair isn't that bad."

"It's bad enough."

He examined my hair carefully, walking around me twice. The second time around he poured us each a cup of coffee and brought them to the bed where I was sitting with my feet hanging over the side. "I used to watch my dad brush my mom's hair. It didn't look so hard."

"It's only bad at first. After the worst of the knots are gone, then it's easy."

"I can see a couple knots in the back. Want me to untangle them?"

Frissons of horror went through me. My boss wanted to brush my hair. My big boss, the one who signed my checks, who could fire me on a whim. There was no way I wanted him to touch me. Anywhere. Except he could see the knots and I couldn't. "Uh… " He handed me a cup of coffee, took the brush from my hand, and turned me around.

"I don't think it'll take long."

It took minutes that seemed like hours. The only thing that made the time bearable was sipping the hot coffee while wearing clothes. When he stopped, he turned me around and checked his work. "Yep, no knots left." He inspected both sides of me, an action that sent such an odd feeling through me that I hid behind my coffee cup. Until it was empty. "I'll take that." He took it and I had nothing else to hide behind. "Want another cup?"

"Yes, please." Why couldn't I keep the squeak out of my voice?

While he got it, I used the brush to pull my hair into a long, neat fall behind my back that I scooped into a rubber band. Then, feeling semi-professional with hair and body in place, I enjoyed my second cup of coffee, complete with enough cream and sugar to qualify it as a cappuccino.

After another cup of coffee each, Ian Macallister shook his head a couple times and moved his shoulders. "I think I'm sober enough to sleep now." He looked at me. "You?"

"Yep." No need to tell him I'd had no liquor.

He left. I locked the door, set the cell alarm for an early wake-up, slid beneath the covers, and waited for sleep to come. Instead, I stared at the blinking smoke alarm and wished I could get Ian Macallister out of my mind. I failed completely. And when I finally slept, I dreamed of my boss, only in my dream he lived at the bottom of a lake with... something. I couldn't make out his companion, I just knew there was one.

Then my alarm went off and it was morning and, yes, the sun was shining. We'd best get going if we wanted to reach that lake and return safely before the next storm hit. And no, we weren't going to inspect some new property as he'd said. Not even to see the lake, pretty as it might be. We were going on a ghost hunt.